KIM KARR

Sexy Jerk

This book is a work of fiction. All names, characters, locations, and incidents are products of the author's imagination. Any resemblance to actual persons, living or dead, locales, or events is entirely coincidental.

Editing:
Nichole Strauss, Insight Editing Services

Interior design & formatting:
Christine Borgford, Type A Formatting

Cover designer:
Michele Catalano-Creative

Cover model:
Andrew Biernat

Photographer:
Wander Aguiar Photography

"What makes you different, makes you beautiful."
~Unknown

Sexy Jerk

My best friend is married.

Everyone I know is married. It doesn't bother me. I like my life the way it is.

Since I'm single though, when my best friend and her husband decide to finally go on their dream honeymoon, she asks me to watch their three-year-old son.

Of course I say yes.

What my best friend neglects to tell me is that I won't be babysitting alone.

Feeling Max might be too much for me to handle, her husband asks his only single friend to help.

Nick Carrington and I have met a couple of dozen times. I've never really given him a second thought—other than to say he's kind of a jerk. Out loud. So he can hear. Sure, he's tall, dark, and handsome. And yes, he has the best ass I've ever seen, and I mean *ever seen* quite literally. You see he mooned me at last year's Fourth of July barbecue because, like I said, he's a jerk.

He always has to be the life of the party.

He's also arrogant.

Imposing.

Rich.

And a playboy.

I'd even go as far as to say he's a manwhore.

Yet somehow before I know it, this manwhore and I are co-parenting. Living under the same roof. Eating meals together and yes, talking.

Don't look at me like that—it's not like I had a choice. Even though I knew every minute would be hell, I had to say yes.

But after two weeks what I didn't expect is that I'd been wrong about him.

That under his smartass exterior, he's actually quite charming.

That his arrogance is actually confidence.

And that the sight of his naked body would do really bad things to me.

So yes, I've misjudged him. And yes, I like him. Really like him. Although there are times I still think he's a jerk . . . I now think he's a sexy jerk.

And I want more of him.

The question is—*does he want more of me?*

One

Tess Winters

FROM THE OUTSIDE, it doesn't look like much. The sign is a bit tarnished. The brick façade is slightly crumbling. And the large picture window is coated in soot.

Still, I am sure beauty is hiding beneath all the dirt and dust.

Opening the old heavy door, I step inside and try to ignore the musty smell. As I glance around, I begin to imagine the possibilities.

Each click of my high heels echoes as I walk. Slowly, I move through the large, open space examining every square inch.

Pristine white walls.

Nice touch.

Old dark wooden floors.

Charming.

Looking up, I flinch at the chaos of the recessed lighting and black painted ceiling. Tapping my chin, I consider my options. Perhaps I will hang a crystal chandelier from one of those wooden beams some day soon, but if I do, it will only be because *I* want it.

However, there absolutely will never be Chateaubriand or

Cognac served here. There will be no JACKETS REQUIRED sign posted on the front door, either. And there absolutely will not be a star chef, whose name appears on the awning, cooking in a gourmet-style kitchen, barking orders and demanding attention.

Even though I'm more than uncertain this is the right place, I know it has to be. It is the one that can work. No, it is the one I have to make work. Truth be told, it is the only one left on the market in this area I can afford.

Armed with this potent knowledge, I glance around once again. This time as my eyes access the imperfect condition of the property with displeasure, I know I have to clear the current state from my mind.

So there are a few cracks in the walls. Uneven floors. And water spots on the ceiling.

Those can all be fixed.

With a little of my own persuasion, I reassure myself it doesn't matter that this isn't a posh landmark Park Avenue building in New York City. It doesn't matter that there will not be valet parking. Or a wait staff. Or reservations. All that matters is that this old accounting office on West Kinzie Street in Chicago will be mine.

And mine alone.

The space isn't big enough for a state-of-the-art kitchen. However, there is plenty of room for the finest of espresso machines, a stove, an oven, and a glistening pastry case. The case can display chocolate croissants, muffins, miniature pastel meringues, and maybe even madeleines—that is if I can find a baker who knows how to make them.

The café can also serve savory offerings like roasted butternut squash soup and a pork club sandwich with pickled eggs, tomatoes, and spicy mayo on sourdough. Hopefully this will encourage the morning crowd to come back for lunch.

There will be no liquor license granted, that I already know because of the location. Although, the realtor tells me I might be able to swing a wine and beer permit. Selling organic wines and craft beers with large molasses cookies in the evening could be fun.

There will be no fine linens or candlelit dinners, but that doesn't mean the place isn't going to be romantic in its own way.

Still, it will never be restaurant royalty.

It will never earn a Michelin star.

It will never be Gaspard—the restaurant I had helped build from the ground up.

And Ansel Gaspard will not be a part of it, nor will he be a part of my life any longer.

And I am okay with that.

One hundred and one days after it all came crashing down, I am finally okay with that.

More than okay with that.

This will be mine.

All mine.

Who knows, maybe someday I'll even offer live music in the evenings. Kind of a Central Perk-like place from the television show *Friends*.

The figure moving behind me jolts me out of my daze. My realtor has walked over to where I had stopped to look out the window. "Do you have any questions, Miss Winters?" he asks.

I glance over my shoulder at him and slide my cold hands into my coat pockets. "It's Tess," I say with a smile as I turn. "And I have just one."

Derrick Williams, the realtor, who is a friend of a friend of a friend, beams at me. "What is it?"

"How soon can you write up the paperwork?"

His brows lift in surprise. "Just like that?"

"Yes, just like that. When can I take occupancy?"

Derrick rushes to pull his iPhone from his breast pocket. "Give me just a minute."

I nod.

After tapping a few buttons, he looks up. "My client can meet you here the day after tomorrow with the lease. I just need to gather some information, if that's all right."

"Yes, of course."

"Great," he says and then exchanges his iPhone for a small notebook. "Will you be using this location as office space or for retail?"

"Neither. I am going to open a gourmet café."

Derrick puckers his lips as if uncertain of my answer. "When you asked about the wine and beer, I just assumed you were looking to open some sort of food store."

"Is a café a problem?" I ask.

"No, no, it shouldn't be."

I furrow my brows. "Shouldn't be?"

"I mean no, not that I am aware of," he responds.

"Okay," I answer skeptically.

He asks me a few more questions, and then finally puts his notebook away. "I just need your driver's license number for the background check."

"Not a problem, but it's from New York."

"That's fine, and if you can provide the first and last months rent at the time of the lease signing, you can take occupancy as soon as March first," he adds.

March first?

March first!

That is so much sooner than I had expected.

That is less than three days from now, not the more than three weeks or three months I had anticipated. I have so much to do. Planning. Permits. Equipment. Fixtures. Contractors. Furniture. Suppliers. Vendors. Décor. Staff. Menus. My mind feels like it's flying.

"Miss Winters? Is everything okay?" Derrick asks.

Taking my hands from my pockets to fish my wallet from my purse, I put a giant smile on my face. "Everything is perfect."

More than perfect.

Two

Tess

AS TWILIGHT HOVERS over the Chicago skyline, the color of the sky reminds me of *his* eyes—stormy gray. My small car can't accelerate fast enough for me to erase the image from my mind. I concentrate on moving through the traffic on Clark Street, changing lanes when I can, in an effort to think of anything else because *he* will not capture anymore of my attention.

After all, I have spent the last six years of my life with him, and thought it would be forever. *Boy, was I wrong.*

As crazy as it sounds, when Ansel Gaspard and I met, I just knew we were going to hit it off.

That day is a day I'll never forget.

It was my first day at the Culinary Institute in New York City. I had recently transferred from the University of Chicago to complete my final year of studying restaurant management at the elite establishment. It was also Ansel's first day. He had moved from France to finish his advanced culinary arts training in the city where he had decided he wanted to live.

He was late for class, and the only seat open was the one next to mine. I looked up. He looked down. When our eyes met, we both knew we had to have each other. I always said he charmed me from his very first 'bonjour'. Not only was he hot, but his French accent left me breathless.

We quickly became an item, and before I even blinked, the year was over. That was when we became business partners. You see, after graduating, Ansel convinced me to stay in the city, and then he convinced me we should open Gaspard together. *"With mind and talent, we can't go wrong,"* he'd said.

Unlike most businesses, startup expenses weren't an obstacle for us because Ansel came from money. Gaining attention, notoriety, establishing ourselves, now those were obstacles. The first two years of Gaspard being in business were tough, both physically and emotionally. Ansel and I worked seven days a week, usually different shifts to keep management coverage. I opened at two and usually left by ten. He came in at four and stayed until closing. Our relationship had always been easy and I didn't think the lack of quality time we spent together mattered. The fact was, I was independent, and I never relied on anyone.

So, I did my thing. He did his. I thought it worked.

Things started looking up for the restaurant after Ansel earned his Michelin star. So much so that two years later, four years after we opened the doors, we were considered one of the best French restaurants in the city, and we had done it together.

Together.

We were a team. At least I thought we were.

Bastard.

My phone rings and the sound jars me from my hostile thoughts. Reaching across the passenger seat, I slip my hand into the front pouch of my purse. When I check the display, I can't help but smile. It is my best friend, Fiona Miller.

She's the girl who moved next door to me in the Chicago suburb of Elmhurst when we were both five. Ever since then we have been stuck together like glue. We've seen each other through so much, and I can honestly say I love her like no one else in my life, except maybe for Max, her son.

"Hi, Fiona," I answer.

"Tessseee," she greets. "You're never going to guess what I'm doing right now."

I glance at the clock on the dash of my new car. Well, new to me. It is only six in the evening. Is she drunk this early? That's not like her at all. "Making dinner?" I guess to appease her. And drinking too much wine, I want to add but don't. Not yet anyway. I need to feel the situation out. See what's up.

"Beeeeeppppp . . . no. The baby already ate, and there will be no further food preparations in this household for anyone by me tonight. Try again."

Okay, I think, something happened, and hence the wine. Just then I hear a noise in the background that sounds like splashing. "Giving Max a bath?" I guess again.

She laughs, but it doesn't sound sincere. "Well, yes, but no. Hell, forget the guessing game, I'll just tell you. I'm walking around the bathroom in my brand new bikini with a giant glass of wine in my hand trying to keep it together. I'd lock myself in here for the next two weeks if the doorknob wasn't broken."

"Fiona, what happened? What's going on?" I ask with concern.

With a sigh, she whisper yells, "Ethan wants to postpone the trip."

I stop at a light. "Oh, no, Fi, why? Did he chicken out about spending the money?"

She gives me a slight laugh. "Believe it or not, no."

"Did something come up at work?"

Ethan has recently become junior partner at his firm and seems to work all the time. "No, believe it or not, it isn't work either," she replies with a sniffle this time.

She's been crying.

"Then why?" I ask. "You've been planning this trip to Fiji for months. It's your dream honeymoon, and Ethan knows it."

Fiona and Ethan are both attorneys. They met while working on a case, on opposite sides. It was not love at first sight. More like hate at first sight. Fiona was an associate at one law firm and Ethan was an associate at another. They spent a lot of time together over a thirty-day period, and somehow ended up between the sheets. Just once, she insisted. Still that was enough for her to accidently get pregnant. Shortly after the discovery, they married, she took a leave of absence from her job, and now almost four years later, they are finally going on their honeymoon. Fiona has been looking forward to this trip for a quite a while.

"Mommy. Mommy. Mommy. Mommy." Max is on repeat again and I have to suppress my chuckle. This is a new phase and Fiona goes mad when he does that.

"Max, what does Mommy say about repeating the same word over and over?" Fiona asks him softly.

"Mommy. Mommy. Mommy. Mommy."

She sighs. "Sorry, Tess. Are you still there?"

The light turns green and I hit the accelerator. "Yes. Now tell me what happened? Why does Ethan want to put the trip off?"

"I don't think I should tell you," she hiccups.

"Fi, tell me," I demand.

Her voice grows low. "Don't be mad."

"Okay, I won't be mad, I promise. Now tell me."

"He's worried Max will be too much for you to handle in your state."

I frown. "In my state?" I say in question.

"You know what I mean."

"In my state!" I repeat loudly.

"Max has been a lot to handle lately, and Ethan's not sure you're up to taking care of Max after everything that happened with Ansel."

"I was going through a break up, Fi, not a break down."

Yes, for a small period of time I might have felt like my world ended. And at the time I thought it had. My life was Gaspard—the restaurant—and it was taken from me. Sure, I had suddenly moved back to Chicago three weeks ago and cried on Fiona's couch for seven days straight. I felt lost. Who wouldn't? I'd spent years giving everything I had to my job. And yes, I might have even refused to go out of the house. And perhaps I had eaten nothing but ice cream for three of those seven days. But that was weeks ago.

Slowly, I'd slipped out of the haze and realized I could do it again. The restaurant that is, not Ansel. This time it would be my way. Simple. Easy. No show. No glitz. No glam.

And I got my shit together.

I moved into my own place, a very affordable studio just west of the South Side. I haven't unpacked, or bought furniture, but those are minor details. I've been busy getting started on my new quest.

Fiona thinks I'm crazy to attempt this alone. She says she knows a guy who would be perfect for me. *"Why not settle down and buy a house with a white picket fence?"* she has said over and over. I put an end to that crazy idea before she could even blurt the guy's name out.

I'm not cut out for relationships.

I can never be what men want me to be.

I've proven that over and over.

Managing the restaurant made me feel like I mattered. Like I was in control. It made me feel like maybe that is who I am.

So, my answer is to be me. Or a version of me that seems closest to who I am, anyway.

That doesn't make me crazy or unfit.

It just makes me closer to *the me* I think I could be. It seems I've moved away from that person over the years.

Besides, putting all of my woes aside, I had planned to watch Max for the two weeks Fiona and Ethan would be gone way before Ansel and I broke up and I moved back to Chicago. I was flying here to stay at her house. If I could handle it then, I could handle it now.

"His words, not mine," Fiona states. "And you said you wouldn't be mad."

"I'm not mad, Fi, but you don't think it's a little late to start second guessing the person you both entrusted to take care of your son in the event of your death? His Godmother. His guardian," I remind her.

"That's what I told him," she whisper yells.

"And?"

"He said he's having cold feet."

I slam the steering wheel. "That's bullshit. He's going on a vacation, not getting married again. He's just using me as an excuse to get out of it for his own reasons, and that is completely unacceptable. Now how about you get Max out of the tub, dry that hot little bikini of yours, and get packed. You are going on your honeymoon tomorrow as planned."

She sighs yet again. "Tess, I don't think I can change Ethan's mind this time. He seems determined to postpone this trip."

Switching lanes, I prepare to make a U-turn. The offices of Fitz, Graham, and Wheeler are only minutes away, and I am going to pay Ethan Miller a visit. "Fi, you might not be able to persuade him, but I guarantee I can."

"Tess, what are you going to do?" she asks hesitantly.

My wheels skid on the black ice as I make the illegal turn. "Why, Fi, what all unstable, broken-hearted women like me do. Put him in his place."

And that I say with a smile.

Three

Tess

THE PRESTON SCHOOL in Lincoln Park is where Max spends three afternoons a week. Even though Fiona stays home, her and Ethan felt Max needed the socialization skills that accompanied attending preschool.

I don't disagree that Max should attend preschool. My reason though is completely different—Fiona needs that time for herself.

Don't get me wrong, the school is the best of the best, and besides, Max does need to be around other children his age.

But Fiona is having a hard time adjusting to staying home, still. She's lonely.

I know she misses her career, but there's more to it. Something is missing from her life. Excitement. Fun. And I think she also misses the attention of a man. The attention of her husband.

Yes, she loves Max with all her heart, but the fact that her husband works all the time isn't making her happy. His political aspirations that take even more of his time from her aren't making her happy. Their non-existent sex life isn't making her happy. Her battery-operated vibrator isn't keeping her satisfied. She really wants this vacation for them. A little me time and we time with her husband to reignite their passion and get their relationship back on track.

And that is what I told Ethan.

To man up and take care of his wife's needs.

I laid it all out on the table. He needed to know. Know his wife was feeling neglected, and not in a selfish way. She just wants a little bit of his attention. And she deserves it.

Those words of wisdom, along with my slightly exaggerated, entirely put together plan to open the café, to prove my mental state was more than stable, was how I convinced my best friend's husband to take his wife on her dream honeymoon.

And it is nothing but the truth.

How could the want-to-be senator argue with that bit of sanity?

They left this afternoon for Fiji to drink fruity cocktails and have lots of sex for the next two weeks.

Today is Wednesday. And on Monday, Wednesday, and Friday, Max spends his afternoons with eleven other preschoolers learning his colors, letters, and even how to speak French.

Crazy, right?

It's no joke.

Very soon my godson might be able to speak better French than me, and I dated a Frenchman for six years. Of course, my Frenchman only liked to talk to me in French when he'd had too much to drink and was extremely horny. That's when the dirty French talk emerged. I didn't care, I found it sexy as hell.

Still, my knowledge of the language is limited to things like, "Je veux ta bouche sur ma bite," or, "I want your mouth on my dick."

Then there was, "Votre chatte a un goût étonnant," or, "Your pussy tastes amazing." And let's not forget the infamous, "I need to be inside you right now," which translated in French is, "J'ai besoin d'être à l'intérieur de toi maintenant." In English it doesn't sound nearly as romantic.

Drunk or not, his words always turned me on. Something about the dirty talk turned me inside out. Too bad it didn't happen that often. Not that I encourage drinking, but . . .

Anyway, don't get me wrong, Ansel liked to fuck. I did too. The problem was I only wanted to fuck him. He, on the other hand, felt compelled to fuck anything in a skirt. I just didn't know it. Shame on me for thinking I should have been enough for him.

Enough time wasted on him.

After spending the afternoon at an industrial interior design center just outside the city limits, I arrive at Max's school promptly at five forty-five.

The teacher is wearing a very nice black pants suit and she has her hair in a perfect chignon. Geez, I thought preschool teachers wore overalls and long dresses. Guess here they break that stereo-type. Anyway, I try to recall her name. It's on the tip of my tongue, but doesn't come to me fast enough.

The teacher looks at me with contempt. "Ms. Winters?"

Curious as to what the look is for, I give her a nod and glance around the room. It is then that I realize Max is the only child left. "I thought pickup time was between five and six Mrs.—?" I let the phrase hang.

"It's Miss Eastling. And yes that is correct," she answers sternly.

"Great, then I'm not late," I reply, and dutifully gather Max and his things.

"But you should know, all the moms pick up promptly at five," she mentions just as I head for the door.

"Well, my name is Auntie Tess, not Mom, so between five and six will have to do over the next two weeks," I reply.

"Auntie Tess. Auntie Tess. Auntie Tess. Auntie Tess." Max repeats over and over as soon as we get in Fiona's BMW SUV.

Hmmm . . . perhaps I had spoken out of turn at Preston, and this is karma's way of calling me a bitch?

I hope not.

Four

Tess

THE QUAINT TREE-LINED street of Hudson Avenue is where Fiona and Ethan's very old East Lincoln Park home is located. Originally built in 1886, the narrow brick building with three floors has a charm that I just love.

Easing down the street, I take a left about ten homes from theirs to circle around to the alleyway where their driveway is positioned.

Spotting the black Range Rover parked there puts me on edge. The chrome wheels and tinted windows immediately give it away. It belongs to Nick Carrington, one of the biggest real estate developers in Chicago. Nick also happens to be Ethan's former college roommate and best friend. Oh, and did I mention, he's Max's Godfather.

What the hell is he doing here?

Last I heard he was in Miami for an extended amount of time working on a really big real estate deal. Then again it isn't like I keep tabs on him. He and I don't exactly get along.

Yes, we've been forced together in the same social settings at least a couple dozen times since Fiona and Ethan met. But to be honest, I've never really given him a second thought—other than to say he's kind of a jerk.

Out loud.

So he could hear.

Many times.

Sure, he's tall, dark, and handsome. And yes, he has the best ass I've ever seen, and I mean *ever seen* quite literally. You see he mooned me at Fiona and Ethan's Fourth of July barbecue last year, which pretty much defines his personality.

He always has to be the life of the party.

He's also arrogant.

Rich.

And a playboy.

Every time I see him, he has a different woman on his arm. I can say this about him—he doesn't discriminate. Tall, short, blonde, brunette, they've all gotten their turn with Chicago's most eligible bachelor. From what I've heard, he just never keeps any of them around long enough to give them a chance.

Plain and simple, he's a manwhore.

And I've had my fill with manwhores. So seeing his vehicle in the driveway isn't making me extremely pleased right now.

Again I ask myself, "Why is he here?"

Unless.

No, please no, don't tell me something happened to Fiona.

Hitting the gas, I floor it into the driveway as fast as I can. Once I put the SUV in park, I hurry to get Max out of his car seat.

Rushing inside with Max on my hip and his gear on my shoulder, I take the stairs up to the main floor two at a time, and come to a screeching halt.

Oh.

My.

God.

Holy shit!

Coming down the stairs is all six-foot-two inches, and I mean all six-foot and two inches of Nick Carrington in his glory.

Wet.

No towel.

Completely naked.

He looks at me, only a little surprised, and mumbles, "Shit," or something like that. I'm not really listening right now. There is so much white noise in my head that I don't think my ears are working properly. Or my hat is on too tight.

Wait.

Ignore that two inches part because he is, well, to be blunt . . . huge.

"Uncle Nick," Max screams in delight, jolting me out of the trance I had fallen into.

"Nick!" I scream in outrage, while at the same time relieved that nothing must be wrong with Fiona or Ethan.

He covers himself with his hands and shrugs.

"Nick! What the hell!" I yell.

"Uncle Nick!" Max exclaims again with glee.

My head jerks in Max's direction. Instead of following suit and covering his eyes like me to shade his vision from the sight of Nick's smooth, tanned, muscular chest, tight six-pack, and well, his huge endowment, the almost three-year-old reaches out for him.

Traitor.

"Hey, Tess. Good to see you," Nick says, seemingly unfazed in the least by his nakedness.

Jerk.

"Nick!" I manage again, beginning to worry I am taking after Max now with the repeating.

Nick lets out a chuckle that really irritates me. "Shit," he says again. "You got up the stairs much faster than I thought you would.

Let me just grab some clean clothes and I can help you with Max's things."

"Uncle Nick. Uncle Nick. Uncle Nick. Uncle Nick," Max keeps repeating, squirming relentlessly for me to let him down.

My eyelids remain squeezed shut, but I need both hands to help with my struggle to keep Max secured to my hip because he has now started to kick his feet. "What are you doing, Nick?" I ask without looking in his direction.

"I went for a run and grabbed a quick shower. Like a dumbass, I left my bag down here with my clean clothes and thought I could mad dash it once I heard the garage door. Guess I was wrong. You don't have to keep your eyes closed. I'm sure you're not going to see anything your French guy Andy isn't equipped with."

Dumbass is right.

Feeling like I've been stabbed in the heart, I give up the struggle with Max and let him down just in time to see Nick's back muscles ripple as he bends to open the large duffle bag on the ground beside his bare feet. "His name is Ansel, not Andy," I correct, "but I'm pretty sure you already know that. And for the record, he's not my guy anymore. We broke up."

Nick raises his gaze, and for the first time I notice just how blue his eyes are. "I'm sorry to hear that. Ethan hadn't mentioned it," Nick says rather sincerely as he pulls on a pair of jeans, opting to go commando.

Not that I notice.

Without bothering to button them, he then grabs for Max who is already by his side. "Hey kiddo," he says, scooping him up and tossing him in the air a few times before setting him on his feet. "What do you say we get these warm clothes off?"

Max giggles and nods his head, taking his own hat off and tossing it to the ground. His hair is a mess, much like Nick's, and I think he knows it because he pulls on his own blond curls to try to make them stand straight on end, more like Nick's. Nick copies him, making his dark hair look somehow put together despite the fact he is fresh out of the shower. Even if I hate to admit it, it is kind of cute to watch their interaction.

As Nick starts to unzip Max's coat, I clear my throat.

Nick looks over at me.

I am standing at the top of the stairs from the lower level and he is still standing across the room near the bottom of the stairs leading to the upper level. It's odd, but neither of us has moved very far.

Are we at a stand off?

"What are you doing here?" I ask again. This time I added the word *here* to be more direct. And yes, I also did that so I wouldn't sound like Max on repeat.

Having already removed Max's coat, Nick shoves Max's hat and mittens in the sleeves and hangs the coat on the banister, all the while glaring at me with a look of utter confusion. "I'm here to help you with Max."

Dumbfounded, I drop Max's things to the floor and take a step forward, pointing my finger at the very large duffle bag. "You're staying here? In this house?"

Nick nods.

"With me and Max?" I clarify, now taking my own hat and coat off because even though it is only twenty degrees outside, it feels like a hundred in here.

Again, he just nods.

"No, no you're not. No way," I insist.

There is a slight rise of his brows. And then he does it again. He nods, like him and I living together is the most normal thing in the world.

Max nods too.

And then Nick sits on the floor and Max copies him, flopping to the ground in a burst of cuteness and landing right in front of

Nick. "Let's take your boots off," Nick says, pointing to Max's feet.

Max points to Nick's bare toes, which I have to admit, are pretty damn sexy. "Socks too," Max says.

Nick laughs. "Socks too." And then he gets to work removing Max's boots.

"Nick," I say calmly this time.

"Tess." He glances up.

"You can't take care of Max. What do you know about kids, other than being a big kid yourself?"

Nick's eyes narrow and he flips me the bird behind Max's back. Okay, I deserved that one. I might have gone too far with that because obviously he is a big part of Max's life. I, on the other hand, haven't lived in Chicago since way before Max was born. To Max, I've just been the visiting auntie. So, what the hell do I know?

"Okay, yes, clearly you can," I concede. "Still, we cannot live in this house together for the next two weeks."

Nick merely grins. "Well, we are, so I guess we can."

It takes all I have to suppress my snarl of rage. "No, we're not."

"Tess, we are. Both Fiona and Ethan have entrusted us with Max. Their son. And I don't plan to disappoint them. And if you take a moment to think about it, I doubt you do either."

Way to put it. "That just sucks," I say rather childlike under my breath. Then add, "You can sleep downstairs on the couch."

Nick laughs again. "It's cold down there. How about we compromise. I'll sleep in the guest room upstairs, but shower downstairs."

I cross my arms in protest. "Fine, but this sucks."

"I heard you the first time. I'm going to wager a bet that Ethan neglected to mention that I would be here."

It hits me then—why Ethan had been so accommodating last night. He must have been working on his back up plan all along. And Nick was it.

"Yes, conveniently he did. And so did Fiona, for that matter,"

I sputter.

"To Fiona's benefit, she didn't know until this morning when I walked in the door to take Max to preschool."

"You dropped him off?" For some reason I just thought Ethan and Fiona had dropped him off before heading to the airport."

"Promptly at eleven. Like I said, I'm here to help."

With my arms still crossed, I keep them there, knowing for some reason my nipples are protruding under the cashmere of my sweater. "This situation still sucks," I mutter.

Nick bends down to kiss Max's little toes, and my heart does the oddest pitter-patter, and then he averts those very blue eyes my way and that pitter-patter speeds up. "Are you worried?" he asks.

Both of Max's feet are bare now, and he jolts up like a jack-in-the-box. Nick follows, and the sight of his long, muscled limbs, and smooth sun-burnished skin curls my fingers, even inside the leather of my gloves. "No, I'm not worried," I say, pulling my gloves off and then turning to head toward the kitchen to prepare Max's dinner. "It's not like I think you'll do anything to me, besides I know self-defense moves."

Nick's laugh is loud. Almost obnoxious. It takes everything I have not to whirl around and scream, *You really are a jerk.* And it's a good thing I didn't scream those words because when I turn around, I find myself laughing equally as hard.

He wasn't laughing at me.

Max has pulled his own long sleeve shirt right over his head. And is pointing to Nick's very bare chest, to the ridges of his ribs, to the muscle that defines his abdomen, and then to his own pudgy little belly.

This is obviously a thing between the two of them.

Copycat.

Admittedly, it's rather cute.

Once the laughter finally comes to an end, and Max is proudly hiccupping and kicking a little soccer ball that Nick has pulled out of his bag, Nick strides into the kitchen, opens the refrigerator, and grabs a beer. "Want one?" he offers with his obviously very strong back to me.

Turning the stove on to warm the small containers of chicken, applesauce, and peas I had already pulled from the freezer, I stare at them. Fiona had pre-made the food, either knowing I'm not that great of a cook, or worried I wouldn't feed him the organic items she insists on. Looking away from the food, I turn my head in Nick's direction and answer with a, "No thank you, I prefer wine."

Surprising me, he doesn't make a smartass remark, instead he pulls a bottle of Pinot Grigio from the refrigerator and sets it on the counter. After reaching for a glass, he pours the wine and hands it to me. "By the way, I wasn't asking if you were worried because I thought you were concerned about what I might do to you. I was asking because I thought you might be worried about what you might want to do to me," he snickers.

I narrow my stare at him and mouth, "Jerk."

Nick just shrugs, takes a sip of his beer, sets the bottle down, and then walks over and grabs his duffle in one hand, and a still hiccupping Max in the other. As he heads up the stairs, he tosses over his shoulder, "I'll give him a quick bath while you get his dinner ready . . . if you don't mind that is."

"That's fine," I concede.

"Oh, and Tess," he says, "Ethan mentioned you aren't much of a cook."

My stare narrows to small slits in my eyes.

"So," he goes on before I can address the comment, "since you were picking Max up, I stopped and got us Chinese for dinner. It's in the warming drawer. Hope you like it."

Just before popping the small containers of Max's food into the steaming water, I call out, "Nick."

This time he looks over his shoulder.

"Thank you."

He gestures with that nod that is really starting to infuriate me, and then says, "After we get Max to bed, I thought we could make a schedule for his care."

He's such a contradiction that it is now my turn to nod, because really, I am at a complete loss for words.

"See, having me around might not suck after all. In fact, you might even like it."

At that, I roll my eyes.

Famous last words.

Five

Nick Carrington

PEOPLE THINK THEY know you by what they observe, read, and hear.

Judgment is easily placed.

A native magazine insists I'm the city's most eligible bachelor, and suddenly women are dying to date me.

Not necessarily a bad thing.

Word spreads on the street that I'm successful because I got lucky, and because of this false rumor my competition neglects to take my emergence seriously.

Again, not necessarily a bad thing.

Tess is no different. She thinks she knows me. That I only care about myself. That I believe the world revolves around me. *That I'm a jerk.*

And for the last three and a half years I've let her believe that. Never bothered to correct her because honestly . . . I just didn't give a big enough shit.

Sure, she is smoking hot.

And yes she is funny, smart, and dare I say witty. And if that isn't almost a perfect match to my bullshit, then I don't know what is.

But she is also judgmental.

And up until yesterday, I never cared that she saw me as nothing more than an irresponsible playboy. Yet the simple fact that she was appalled she had to co-babysit Max with me, that she was skeptical that I could even take care of him, now that pissed me off.

Who is she to judge me in that way?

And seriously, why am I actually giving a shit now? Because what she sees, what she believes to be true, isn't who I really am?

I'm not a playboy. Not by the true definition. Or at least I don't see myself that way.

I don't have a different woman in my bed every morning and every night. I'm happy with their bed once or twice during the week, but as soon as they start wanting more, it's time to move on.

I might not be a playboy, but shit, I am a hot-blooded man who likes women.

As in plural.

Not multiples, not together, don't get me wrong.

Just not any single one for too long.

It isn't that I don't care about them . . . it's just I prefer not to get attached.

Hence the many that have been in my life.

Let's be real . . . attachments to women only bring heartache. I saw what happened to my old man firsthand when my mother left us to go back to her previous life—left me, my father, and my baby brother. He was a broken man. Sure, he did the best he could to raise his two boys, but he was never the same after she left. He was somehow absent even when he was around. Then again, he was always tired. And I got it. He worked two construction jobs to support us.

When I was younger I helped raise Lucas. When I was old

enough, I helped my old man on job sites, and helped raise Lucas. Even after I left for college, I still helped raise Lucas by coming home on weekends.

Things were tough back then.

I was an eleven-year-old raising a one-year-old.

A twelve-year-old raising a two-year-old.

A fifteen-year-old raising a five-year-old.

You get the picture.

I had no childhood so to speak of.

Sing me a song.

Feel sorry for me.

Fuck that.

That's bullshit.

I did what had to be done.

Besides, the past is just that, the past. Everyone gets over it. My father retired two years ago and now lives in sunny Florida where he scouts property for me. He's happy, and as far as I know, never gives my mother a second thought.

Lucas, on the other hand, is a sophomore in college at Notre Dame. He's the quarterback for their football team, and has way too many women on speed dial. Then again, he, like me, has mommy issues. And I guess, he, not unlike me at his age, thinks he's hot stuff.

But who am I to say anything, especially since he is content, for now, anyway. He lives with me when he's not attending college, and wants to move far away from where we grew up after he graduates.

Sometimes bad turns to good.

And sometimes good turns to shit.

You just never know.

The only thing you can count on is that everything changes. Apparently, even my attitude, because I'm trying to justify myself *to myself.*

What the fuck?

Moving past the bullshit in my head, I open my email and compose a quick message to my buddy Ethan.

To: Ethan Miller
From: Nick Carrington
Subject: You Suck

Nice one man. Next time how about a heads up before you send me into the lion's den? By the way, Max is fine, and you suck.

After hitting send, I read a few incoming work emails.

Unable to concentrate for long, I minimize the window and stare at my computer screen. It's two in the afternoon, and on any normal day I would have slayed a few dragons and climbed a couple of mountains by now. Instead, I'm sitting here twiddling my thumbs, unable to get my head in the game.

Just then my intercom buzzes. It's my assistant and she's probably going to ask me if I've signed the contracts Ethan sent over before he left yesterday for the Miami land deal. The ones that are on my desk and I've only glanced at. Fuck. "Yes, Carrie?" I answer.

"Mr. Carrington, I hate to bother you, but do you have those contracts signed yet? I'd like to send them out and then, if you don't mind, I was hoping I could leave early. The school called and my daughter has a fever."

Swiveling in my chair, I look through the glass at the snow falling down and notice Jackson Boulevard is covered with it. "I'm still reviewing the contracts, but go ahead and leave. I'll finish reviewing them this afternoon and you can send them back to Mr. Miller's office first thing in the morning."

"Are you sure, sir?"

I turn back in my chair. "Yes, I'm sure. It's really not a problem."

"Thank you," she says.

"No need to thank me, Carrie. Now go."

Carrington Development is a small business located on the tenth floor of a large office complex in Printer's Row. It consists of me—the CEO, Carrie—my assistant, two field scouts—Hayden and Ash, and their assistants—Natasha and Tammy. It's small, and I like it that way. Family-like. Hayden has a new baby with his girlfriend, Allie. Ash is single, so he and I often grab a beer after work. Natasha and Tammy are both married. Like I said, the operation is small and I like it that way.

The truth is, I made my first million right out of the gate because I understood Chicago, not because of my size, or because I got lucky. I knew Printer's Row would be ripe for retail and restaurant expansion as soon as the area south of Magnificent Mile and River North became too oversaturated. So I bought and bought and bought, and waited. And boom . . . the area blew up like firecrackers on the Fourth of July. That was eight years ago, and I haven't stopped doing what I do—scouting, buying, developing, and waiting.

Sifting through the pages on my desk, I read Ethan's notes first. He's worried the price is too steep for me and will put my other business deals at risk due to low cash flow if the deal takes too long to go through. "Risk, buddy," I write. "It's the name of the game."

Then I spend the next couple of hours reviewing the bid, the terms, the contingencies. This is for a very large parcel of vacant land outside the Miami city limits. Right now the area is desolate. I want to develop it. Homes, condos, and restaurants.

Why?

Because that is what developers do.

What I do.

I buy land, finance real estate deals, build or have builders build projects, lease out buildings I own, create, imagine, control, and orchestrate the process of development from the beginning to the end. I take the risk—and receive the reward.

And that is who I am.

Not a playboy, but a businessman who works hard and plays hard.

There my mind goes again—right back to Tess and what she thinks of me.

Without overthinking it, I grab for my cell phone and hit Tess's number. We'd done the number exchange gig last night. And yes, I made sure she knew it wasn't for sexting.

Shit, I really am a jerk sometimes.

Today is her day with Max. Mine is tomorrow. Splitting the weekend into shifts seemed like the best way to handle the time. We haven't planned next week yet. That might have been pushing the amicability between the two of us a little too far. After agreeing on the schedule, we both went to our rooms by nine. Separately, of course. I did suggest we bunk together. She flipped me off.

In the end, Tess took the master bedroom, and I took the upstairs spare, as was agreed upon. Again, there were surprisingly no issues there, although I think she would have preferred I had agreed to take the couch in the basement.

"Hello," she answers. Her voice is low, almost sultry, and the sound makes my cock pulse.

What the hell?

Ignoring what's happening below my waist, I hit the speaker button and lean back in my chair. "Hey, it's me. I just wanted to check on you and Max."

"Hang on," she whispers.

"Yeah, sure."

"Okay, sorry. Max and I were watching television and we both fell asleep," she laughs.

"You let him fall asleep on the couch?" I ask in mock horror. "At four o'clock in the afternoon?" I add a little louder.

"I know, right? It's so against the parenting rules. Promise me you won't tell Fi, but he wouldn't take a nap, so I didn't make him, and then about ten minutes ago he conked out."

"What do I get if I keep quiet?"

Shit, am I flirting with her?

"Depends on how good you are."

Shit, is she flirting back?

"Oh, I can be very good," I reassure her.

She laughs. "Then I'll save the gold stickers for you, big boy."

Okay, not flirting, but pulling my chain.

"But I really like the silver ones," I tease like an adolescent, then change topics. "Anyway, I'll be headed that way in about an hour. What do you feel like eating for dinner? I can pick it up on my way."

It was time to change gears.

"You mean I get to pick something, and you'll get what I ask for?"

Picking up my pen, I sign the contract. "Yes, Tess. That is what I said."

"Oh, it's just that at Fiona and Ethan's engagement party when you asked me if I wanted a drink and I said yes, I'd have a glass of champagne, you brought me a bottle of beer."

I slip the contract in the envelope. "Tess, what do you want for dinner?"

She ignores my question. "Nick, do you remember that?" she taunts, not leaving well enough alone.

"I do, Tess, and just so you know, the beer was for me, the bartender was uncorking a new bottle of champagne just for you. But before I could tell you that, Andy showed up to whisk you onto the dance floor, and well, let's just say I drank the entire bottle of 2006 Dom Perignon all by myself."

She's silent for a few moments and doesn't even correct me about her Frenchman's name. "You bought a $200 bottle of champagne for me?"

"Yes, I did."

"But we'd just met."

"And you were my best friend's fiancé's best friend. What can I say, I wanted to make a good impression."

"That was really sweet."

Sweet?

Sweet!

Is that pity I hear?

Fuck that.

I'll give it to her straight. "No, trust me, sweet wasn't my intention. The truth is you looked hotter than fuck in that little black dress and I really wanted to get into your panties, before I knew you were attached that is. Obviously, Ethan tends to leave pertinent information off the table."

She's quiet for a beat. "You know, Nick, can you ever leave well enough alone? Do you always have to assure that you come out looking like a total asshole?"

I flinch. "That's what I do best, baby."

"You're such a jerk. Thanks for reminding me of that. I'd be happy with any pasta dish, no meat, if you can manage it without having to stop and get your dick wet."

"Classy Tess, don't kiss Max with that mouth."

"Ugggghhhhh," she sighs and then the line goes dead.

Shit, if that was me trying to show her there's more to me than what she sees, I think I need to stop trying so hard.

Or maybe all together.

Six

Nick

THERE ARE MANY perks to running your own company. Making your own hours, being your own boss, and not being accountable to anyone. Yet right now the fact that I have my own personal gym beside my office is the only one that matters.

I'm sweating and biting back grunts as I run like hell, trying to escape my own destructive self. She's not wrong. Why didn't I just leave well enough alone?

When I first met her, I was trying to impress her, and not only because I wanted in her pants. But also because I was attracted to her personality and for some strange reason wanted to get to know her.

I run faster.

Faster still.

Really, what the hell was wrong with me back then?

What was I thinking?

She's a little too uptight.

Bitchy even.

Judgmental.

Complicated.

Not at all the type of woman I like to fuck.

Out of breath, I start to slow my pace.

Why am I still thinking about her?

The treadmill beeps three point five miles in twenty-four minutes, my fastest time in years. Lifting my shirt, I pat my face and then gulp my water.

I know why—there's something about her.

A reason I've gone out of my way to get her attention every time we've been in the same room.

What that reason is, I don't even want to spend the time considering. It can't end well for her, or me. Especially me, because even after hitting the punching bag and then running my ass off, trying to figure this out has only left me rock hard.

On the plus side, by the time I hit my private shower, the only thing on my mind is why the fuck am I so horny? It's like I'm a teenage boy.

My brain might not be functioning properly but one thing is clear—I can't show up at Fiona and Ethan's place with a raging hard-on. And I certainly can't be in Tess's presence with *one*, especially not all evening.

What if she noticed?

What if she didn't?

Fuck me.

Feeling . . .

Eager.

Bold.

Hot-blooded.

That is just a disaster waiting to happen.

I need to take care of this situation right now.

Jerking off at the office isn't something I normally do, but today

I need to make an exception.

Sitting on the long bench in the middle of the marble bathroom, I pull my track pants down and kick them and my sneakers off. Running my hand down my stomach, I wrap my fingers around my dick and think of how good it would feel to be inside her.

Soon enough, I find myself lying back. As I stare at the ceiling, I pump slowly from my balls to the tip of my cock, once, twice, three times. And suddenly I'm thinking of the noises she might make when I touch her clit and then rub it over and over, or whether or not she'll scream my name when I fuck her hard and fast.

My breathing comes in short bursts as adrenaline pumps through my veins. Out of nowhere, I start to wonder how her wetness might taste—on her tongue, in her mouth, and around her sweet pussy. I press my heels into the ground and push my hips up. My grip grows tighter as I pump my fist harder, faster.

Up.

Down.

Up.

Down.

Again and again.

After a few minutes, I'm on the edge, almost there, but I slow my hand to prolong the pleasure. But then thoughts of her straddling me so she can thrust her hips into mine, rush my need for release. All too soon I'm coming. I arch my back and tip my head, letting the feeling absorb me.

Overtake me.

Own me.

Minutes later I rise from the bench to hop in the shower. Once under the warm spray, I refuse to put a face to the woman's body I just imagined in my mind and used to make myself come.

Because if I think too hard about it, I'm afraid I know whose face it was.

And more than likely . . . she'd slap me if she found out about the very dirty thoughts I was having starring her.

Not fuck me.

Seven

Tess

THE WORLD IS made up of many different kinds of business people. Suits. Khakis. Take charge. Cower down. Go with the flow.

But the bullying type is simply unacceptable.

In fact, there should be laws against this kind of behavior. I give him a sideways glance and see his smirk. There definitely should be laws against it. What this big shot is trying to do is completely unethical and downright underhanded.

I really wish I had done my research before coming to the agreed upon appointment to sign my new restaurant lease, because if I had, I would have canceled. But with everything happening so fast, I neglected to notice whom exactly I would be meeting.

He's a man with a reputation around Chicago.

And not a good one.

Word on the street is that he is a slumlord.

A down and dirty businessman.

Ruthless.

With a narrowed stare, I look my potential new landlord right in the eyes. "I am not signing this lease until you change the monthly lease payment back to the one advertised, and I might add, the previously agreed upon amount."

Pokerfaced, Mathias Bigelow shifts his gaze from the clipboard in his hands over to me, and then stares at me deadpan. "Ms. Winters, the advertised monthly rate was for retail space, not a restaurant."

"But I told Derrick what the space would be used for."

"Derrick," he grits, "is a realtor, and has no decision-making authority in my business."

I have to tread lightly. This man owns a rather large percentage of the properties in River North and is rumored to be involved with organized crime. Figures I'd get stuck with him. "I don't understand why it matters what I plan to use the space for."

Pardon my language, but this dick in a suit doesn't impress me with his business savvy when he indicates to the space we are standing in and says, "Would you like me to explain why it matters, doll?"

Trying hard not to roll my eyes, I answer with what I believe to be an intelligent response. "Yes, Mr. Bigelow, I would because the lease is triple net, and therefore there are no additional expenses out of your pocket."

His face turns red and I think he is getting angry. "Turning this old accountant's office into a restaurant is going to require renovations, extensive renovations, and although the money is not coming out of my pocket, you will be limiting the future revenue streams of this location when you vacate the property."

Now irritation starts to flare beneath my skin. "That makes absolutely no sense. If anything, I'm providing the potential to improve it, not reduce it."

Taking two giant steps toward me, he closes in on me—intentionally moving into my personal space. "Look doll, you either sign the contract or you don't. It's no skin off my back either way, but stop wasting my time."

Whereas Nick in a suit is all smooth and polished, this guy looks rough around the edges even in expensive pinstripes.

Odd thought, I know.

But then Mathias Bigelow takes another step, and his closeness causes my pulse to leap erratically with fear. Effectively banishing all my thoughts about anything except the situation I am in.

When he takes another step toward me, I can smell the foul odor of his cologne, and I am forced to take a step back. He in turn, steps toward me again, caging me against the wall with his free arm.

Somehow I manage to suppress my snarl of rage.

Barely.

How dare he try to intimidate me?

Moving way past fear now, I grit my teeth and go on the attack. "Your shady business tactics won't work with me, Mr. Bigelow."

"Shady." He tips his head back and laughs.

"Yes, shady. You baited me in here, and now you want to switch the deal."

Somehow he moves even closer. "Are you accusing me of trying to pull a scam?"

Now my nerves are back, and I swallow before nodding.

"Do you know who I am?" he bites out.

As if his cologne doesn't smell bad enough, the smell of his coffee breath is vile. The combination is making me sick. My stomach becomes a nervous flutter. I want to get away from him. For a brief moment, I consider pushing him back. But I know I won't be able to budge him, so I don't. There's no way I am giving him that kind of satisfaction. Instead, I answer, "Yes," again, and then add, "I'll sign for the agreed upon amount only."

He merely grins. "And I'll say it one more time, a little slower so you understand, there was no viable, binding prior agreement. This," he raises the hand with the clipboard and at the same time, lowers the arm caging me in, "is the only agreement there is."

I look down at the skirt and knee-high boots I opted to wear and then across to the door, and wonder should I decide to run, if I can make it.

And if I do, will he chase me?

Catch me?

Hold me in his grip?

Not wanting to risk an altercation, I square my shoulders and purse my lips. I can act tough, too.

As if sensing I plan to hold my ground, that he will not intimidate me, he pulls the stapled packet of papers from its holder. Once free, he shoves them at me. "I'll give you until Monday to decide, after that, this place is back on the market. And even with the increased price, you won't find a cheaper place for rent."

Damn him, he's right.

Still, I have my principles and will not be bullied. With shaky fingers I take the papers and stare at him, steady, unwavering. I refuse to show him any fear, or like a lion, he'll prey on it.

Finally he steps back, allowing me room to pass. "Goodbye," I say, willing my trembling voice to remain steady.

He grabs my upper arm, tightly, as I move past him. "You have until Monday," he reminds me, and then lets me go.

When I approach the door, all I can think is, *I showed him.* I am woman hear me roar. As I open the door, all I can think is, *I really need a drink.* But then, as the door closes behind me, all I can think is . . . *I am not sure if I am lucky . . .*

Or screwed.

Eight

Tess

DINNER CONSISTS OF a big bowl of popcorn and a glass of wine.

Over the last three months, this has become habit. And I rather like the ease of popping a bag into the microwave and then uncorking a bottle.

Truth be told, I might have gone to culinary school, but I'm not much of a cook. While I had exceled in restaurant management, food preparation courses weren't my forte. Honestly, I've just never loved cooking.

With my sweatpants on and my brown hair twisted in a knot on top of my head, I turn on the fireplace and blow my bangs from my eyes. My hair is in bad shape. I really could use a bang trim.

The ill state of my hair aside, I sit at the kitchen island with my laptop in front of me and begin to peruse alternative properties for rent. Any of the places within a semi-decent distance of Magnificent Mile are all way too expensive. Besides, more than likely Mathias Bigelow owns them, and God knows what his markup or punishment tax will be for me to rent an alternate one of his other properties.

I take a sip of wine and start adding up the costs to renovate the property I'm interested in, and then the increased monthly lease payments the ruthless bastard wants to charge me. The amount is almost doable. Almost. So close that it's like a tease. So close and yet so far. I simply don't have the money to stretch myself that thin. And I have to say, it's probably a good thing. I don't scare easy. I pride myself on the fact I can take care of myself. Still, he made me nervous.

And with that thought in mind, I realize I'm right back where I started two weeks ago when I started looking around . . . nowhere with nothing.

By the time I hear Nick's Range Rover pull into the driveway, that one glass of wine has somehow turned into three, my worries have quadrupled, and the popcorn bowl is nearly empty.

Nick had taken Max over to Jace Bennett's house right after pre-school pickup. Jace is Ethan and Nick's college buddy.

It's a Friday night tradition for Max.

You see, Jace is recently widowed. He lost his wife of seven years last year to a tragic illness. Not only has he been left a widower at the age of thirty, but he is also a single father to a little girl about six months younger than Max. Let me tell you, Scarlett is the cutest red-head you've ever seen, and she is the spitting image of her mother.

Jace owns Flirt Enterprises, a huge conglomerate of social media dating sites. From what Fiona has told me, between his job and his daughter, Jace has no time left for himself. Knowing exactly how that feels, she takes Scarlett on Friday nights so that the boys can watch a hockey game, shoot some hoops, or just sit around and drink beers.

Nick, previously unbeknownst to me, is obviously a part of the *boys*, and decided not to cancel Friday night altogether. But rather, he went to his friend's house to spend the evening with him and the kids. I have to admit, spending his Friday nights with married men isn't very playboy like.

He's such a contradiction.

Nice when you thought he wasn't.

Helpful when you had no idea he even knew the definition of the word.

What is it they say—don't judge a book by its hard, chiseled, exterior? Well, not quite, but something like that.

"Hey," Nick says softly as he comes up the stairs. Max is already in his pajamas and sound asleep resting his head on Nick's shoulder.

"Hey," I respond quietly, jumping to my feet and almost fall over from the wave of dizziness that hits me. "Let me help you."

Nick shakes his head as he crosses the room. "I got this."

Wanting to assist in removing Max's outerwear, but wondering if I can actually make it up the stairs without stumbling, I decide to sit back down and will the spinning room to stop. I know I'm not drunk. Two glasses of wine and then some isn't enough to intoxicate me.

Nick's strides are quick, and he is up the stairs even quicker.

I close my laptop and shut my eyes, pressing the heels of my palms to my forehead in order to concentrate on gaining my stability.

Minutes pass, and then suddenly the overhead lights flick on. I hadn't realized I'd been sitting in the dark. I move my hands away from my face and blink. My vision blurs and then finally clears.

"Rough night?" Nick asks, taking his coat off and hanging it in the closet near the front door.

"Shitty day," I tell him honestly, and quickly add, "But the night hasn't been so bad."

He's standing beside me in a moment and pointing to the bottle. "I can tell," he says with a smirk. "Mind?"

Surprised he drinks wine, I fight a smile as I push it his way. "Help yourself."

When he reaches for a glass from the cupboard, I can't help but notice how long and lean he is. I've seen his bare torso, I've seen his bare ass, but I've obviously never paid enough attention to how good he looks in suit pants and a white shirt.

Pouring the last of the wine into first my glass and then his own, he dips his chin toward the empty bottle. "So, tell me Tess," he says, in that authoritative manner I used to think was condescending, but now know is just the way he speaks, "why was your day so shitty?" The note of concern in his tone strangely makes me feel like my blood is on fire.

Ignoring this very wrong illicit reaction, I glance up a little too fast and have to grab the island I'm sitting at for support.

Like lightning speed, his glass is down, he has one hand on my shoulder, and the other lifting my chin to look into my eyes. "Hey, Tess, are you okay?"

It's odd but there is this hot, thick feeling inside me that I become aware of almost instantly when his warm skin touches mine. I write it off as too much wine. "Yes, I'm fine. I think I'm just tired."

Letting go of my shoulder, he points to the nearly empty bowl beside me. "Have you eaten anything besides popcorn today?"

Feeling like a fool, I suddenly know why I'm out of sorts. Obviously drinking on an empty stomach is very irresponsible of me, and I have to own up to my stupidity. "No, I haven't," I admit. "But I'm fine now."

Instead of chastising me, or worse, calling me on my irresponsibility, like I probably would have done if the tables were turned, he simply responds with, "Yes, I can see that," and then strides toward the refrigerator.

Curious as to what he is doing, I twist in my stool. "How was your night?"

Bending, he rummages through the contents before him. "It was a good time. We ordered pizza, the kids played, and Jace and

I watched hockey."

"Sounds fun. It certainly looked like Max enjoyed himself."

Setting a carton of eggs, a bag of cheese, and a gallon of milk on the counter beside the stove, Nick glances over at me. "Are eggs okay?"

More than a bit surprised by his question, I start to protest, "You don't have to cook—"

"Tess, how do you like your eggs?" Nick asks, cutting me off.

Somewhat bewildered, I stare at him. Not sure how to answer that. It's weird, but in all the years I was with Ansel, I don't think he ever asked me what I preferred to eat. I always just ate whatever new recipe he had decided to try out.

The skillet clanks as it hits the stovetop. "Do you want them fried or scrambled?" he presses.

It takes me a moment, but finally I answer him. "Scrambled, please."

With a nod, Nick grabs for a glass bowl.

"How's Jace?" I ask, still surprised he's cooking for me.

Nick shrugs as he cracks the eggs. "Honestly, not great. He's struggling to do everything that needs to be done, and refuses help."

My heart hurts for Nick and Ethan's friend. I can't imagine what he is going through. "Maybe he just wants to keep busy," I suggest.

"I'm sure of that, but he can't keep going at the pace he is for much longer. He gets up, takes Scarlett to a daycare near his office, goes to work, leaves the office by six to pick her up, and once she is in bed, he works until God knows what hour. I swear, the dude never sleeps."

I watch Nick with an odd curiosity as he competently whisks the milk in his egg mixture, shakes in some salt and pepper, and then adds a handful of cheese. He knows what he's doing. There is no show, or fancy moves though. It's all done quick and efficiently, with the intent to get to the finished product. "Have you suggested he hire a nanny to help with Scarlett?" I ask.

Nick pours the contents of the bowl into the hot skillet and starts to whip the liquid around with a fork. "Me?"

"Yes, you. Maybe someone needs to let him know it's okay if he can't do everything himself."

"No, I haven't, but I'm sure Fiona must have."

"But he's your friend, so maybe if you suggest it, he'll at least consider the idea," I say optimistically.

Nick smirks at me as he puts some bread in the toaster. "Maybe."

"What?" I ask.

"When did you become little miss sunshine?"

I put my hand to my chest. "I beg your pardon, but I have always been a glass half full kind of girl."

With a snicker, Nick scoops the eggs onto two plates.

"I have," I stress.

The toast pops up. "Whatever you say."

"Nick, I'm serious."

"I'm sure you are," he mumbles under his breath.

"I am."

His smirk remains in place as he grabs the hot slices of bread and quickly drops them to the plates. "Do you remember the night," he says, waving his hand as if he burned it, "of Fiona and Ethan's rehearsal dinner," he goes on, "when I suggested we take the Polar Bear Plunge and you shot me down?"

Torn between watching him make me something to eat and arguing with him, I decide why not do both. "Yes, I do remember, and the idea was just ludicrous."

"But it wasn't."

"Yes, it was."

"Tell me why, Tess?"

This takes me a moment and I feel slightly tongue-tied when I try to explain it. "Just because Ethan and Fiona were taking the plunge, didn't mean we should all strip down to our underwear and jump in the freezing water to take the plunge too."

"But why not? It was funny, and a fantastic idea," he says as he butters the toast.

"Because," my voice raises, "it was stupid, and more than likely we'd all catch cold."

Nick raises a brow. "This said by the glass half full kind of girl."

I say nothing. He has a point. Perhaps in hindsight maybe whenever he's been around I have been somewhat of a Debbie Downer.

With a plate, silverware, and napkin in each hand, he walks toward me. I can't help but notice how his muscles ripple beneath his crisp, white shirt. How his biceps bulge when he moves his arms. The shape of his forearms showing beneath his rolled up sleeves. How square and strong his shoulders are.

While staring at me, he sets everything down.

I find myself staring back into those brilliant blue eyes that must capture the attention of every woman he looks at.

He pushes one of the plates closer to me. "Stop staring and start eating," he commands.

"Yes, sir," I joke, ignoring the fact he caught me, because after all, he was staring first.

Nick raises one sexy brow. "Will you call me master if I get you some juice?"

The moment ruined, as usual, I purse my lips and roll my eyes. "Dream on."

Despite my behavior, he pours us each a glass of juice. Once he sits down, he looks at me, as if waiting for me to comment.

As soon as I finish chewing the bite of eggs of my mouth, I blurt out, "These are really good."

Nick lifts a piece of toast to his mouth. "Eggs, grilled cheese, and spaghetti and meatballs are my specialties."

"I'm impressed," I respond with sincerity.

Wiping his mouth with a napkin, he says, "Oh, yeah, why?"

"I just never thought a wealthy, eligible bachelor like you would know the first thing about cooking."

He laughs. "I practically raised my younger brother, and at the time my father barely made enough to put a roof over our heads, let alone have enough money for me to buy much when it came to food."

Forking some more eggs, I pause. "Where was your mother?"

His eyes flicker. "She left us to go back to her first husband when Lucas was just a baby. I was ten."

My preconceived notion that he was a trust fund baby suddenly seems ridiculous. Why hadn't Fiona told me? I guess I'd never asked. When had I concocted that misconception in my mind? Perception I suppose. Boy, was I wrong. "I'm sorry, I honestly had no idea."

Nick shrugs. "I did what I had to do. It's not like I could leave a little boy to fend for himself. Now finish your food, Tess."

I give him a nod and finish the eggs and toast, realizing just how very hungry I am with each and every bite.

Too bad that hunger doesn't seem to be waning.

It's as I watch Nick drink his juice, pick up his fork, and chew his food, that I realize I'm not sure it's food I'm starved for.

What the hell?

Nine

Tess

NICK IS A jerk.

Nick is a jerk.

Nick is a jerk.

I repeat this over and over in my head as I finish my food, but it doesn't seem to stick because honestly, I'm not so sure he is. There's more to him than I've paid attention to. More to him than he lets on. A lot more to him.

Hmmm.

Once my plate is almost clean, I slide it forward. "I can't eat another bite."

Nick practically puffs out his chest, looking very pleased with himself. Of course he is. Did I say there was more to him? What I meant was a whole lot more arrogance.

Just as I'm about to roll my eyes, he suddenly stands. "Come with me," he beckons, in that dominating tone of his that normally drives me mad. Tonight though, I'm only mildly annoyed by it, and even forget the eye roll all together.

Slowly, and with a slight hesitation, I get to my feet. When I don't move fast enough, he urges me forward.

What?

Does he think he's going to send me to bed like a child?

I'm about to turn to tell him off, to remind him he's not here to babysit me, when he places a firm hand on my back, and I'm silenced where I stand. That thing happens again. The thing where my body feels like it's on fire. I swear even my cheeks feel a little flushed from the flames. The non-existent ones.

Trying not to show my ridiculous schoolgirl reaction to his touch, I square my shoulders as he guides me into the living room. "What are you doing?" I finally manage to ask.

"Getting us both a well-deserved brandy."

My eyes widen. "Ethan's *only for certain occasions* brandy?"

"The very one."

I rub my hands together in excitement. "He's only offered me a glass once." And that was when I showed up on Fiona's doorstep a broken mess and told her Ansel and I were over, but I don't tell Nick that part.

The story goes—Ethan's grandfather was a liquor salesman, and during a business trip to the Soviet Union many, many years ago, he managed to purchase a case the very famous Jubilee Brandy of 1967. Remaining bottles of this production run are highly sought after and Ethan has six of them.

"Count yourself lucky," Nick laughs. "I've known Ethan for almost ten years and the stingy bastard has only shared two glasses with me over that entire span of time. The first time when he found out he was going to be a father and the second was the night Jace's wife died."

Interesting.

What is the common factor that solicits the offering?

Once we cross the threshold to the living room, Nick heads to the bar cart where the crystal decanter is kept, and I head toward the couch in front of the fireplace.

I sit and watch as the actual flames from the fireplace lick their way upward. I can't help but feel like that is what is happening to me right now. There's a fire inside me, and for some crazy reason, Nick is stoking it with each touch, each glance, each word.

I can't explain it.

Too much wine is the only answer.

When Nick hands me the large brandy snifter with a small amount of amber colored liquid inside it, I try to expel the feeling and find myself taking a healthy sip of the liquor to help me do so.

"Now, Tess," Nick says with a speculative look my way.

"Yes, Nick," I answer, and it's then that I notice he's slid his long, lean body onto the couch not that far away from me. I take him in. He has an ankle on one knee, his glass resting on his thigh, and I swear he looks different than I've ever seen him. Sure, he still looks so very confident, so very in control, but he also looks so very male. Glancing over at him makes the heat inside me spread like wildfire. And then, all of sudden, an anticipation I can't explain emerges as I wait for him to speak.

The brandy glass has just barely left his lips when he does. "Tell me why your day was so shitty?"

Surprised he remembers I mentioned that, and more surprised he even cares, I find myself opening up to him. I quickly tell him the entire story about how I almost found my new café a home. Without thought. Without thinking about what it is Nick does for a living. Without realizing he might know Mathias Bigelow. Be his friend, even.

Pausing before I get to the end of my story to take another sip of my drink, I watch as Nick's feature's draw together. His eyes grow cold. His jaw tightens. And his forehead creases.

Crap.

I now really do think Mathias and him are friends. And Nick is growing angry as my story goes on because I assume he thinks I'm exaggerating it.

After a long pause, Nick seems to force his words out. "Are you telling me you met him, *by yourself*, earlier this evening?"

It's not really a question, though. It's more like an accusation.

I nod, not sure if I should stop or continue.

"And," he snaps, as if I am the one who had done wrong by meeting the man.

Angered that his reaction is so visceral, that it seems he has sided with Mathias before even hearing me out, I go on if only to prove to him I was not the shady one.

When I get to the part where Mathias invaded my personal space, I don't tell him I was worried about my well-being. I don't tell Nick, though, not because I am uncertain about his relationship with Mathias Bigelow, but rather because what happened makes me look weak. And the one thing I never want to be is weak, especially in front of a man.

My father was a man of God and believed strongly that a dutiful wife did as she was told. My mother believed the same and never spoke up. Perhaps if she'd spoken up, if she hadn't been so weak, her and my father would still be alive. She didn't want to go on the mission trip to Nigeria, but he insisted. She said it was dangerous. He said they'd be fine. They were killed two days after arriving by a local terrorist organization.

Shutting out the pain, I finish the story by telling Nick I strode out of the rental space without signing anything and headed back here. Then I add, "And I'd been sitting where you found me at the island ever since, mulling everything over."

A low hiss escapes Nick's lips. "Did he touch you? Hurt you in anyway?"

Immediately, I glance away. I don't want any weakness to slip through my already cracking façade because no, he didn't physically hurt me, he just scared me, and that angers me. Really angers me.

"Tess, look at me."

Though his tone is gentle, there is no mistaking the command in his voice. I'm not accustomed to obeying men, and yet, I give him what he wants, and look his way.

Nick's gaze is hard. "Did he?" he repeats.

I shake my head. "No, but he did get really close to me. Close enough that he gave me cause to never want to meet with him alone again."

Everything about Nick goes stiff. "That son of a bitch!"

Without thought, I reach out and place my hand on his thigh. "Nick, really, I'm fine."

The doubt remains evident in his stare.

Through the thumping beat of my heart, I try to find the right words. I have to remove my hand from his leg to do so. It's as if the illicit touch was almost too much to stay focused on the conversation. "To be honest," I tell him, "I'm just pissed at myself for allowing myself to be put in a situation like that. I'm normally much more careful about who I meet with and where."

Nick mutters something under his breath that I can't comprehend. His expression is practically murderous as he shifts his gaze from where my hand had been mere moments ago up to my face.

"Nick?" I whisper, wondering what he is thinking.

There is fire in his brilliant blue eyes, and he looks like he might explode at any second. "You have to give me a minute," he mutters.

Not quite understanding his disposition, I do so anyway.

He visibly inhales and exhales through his nose as if trying to calm himself in what I perceive to be a much-practiced manner.

I find his coping method interesting. Different than I'd have thought. I watch him for the second time tonight. He really is a beautiful man.

Dark and brooding—yes.

Authoritative—yes.

Arrogant—absolutely.

Yet, it doesn't stir fear inside me. No, not at all. In fact, right now, the only thing I feel is safe. Safe, in that he would never do what Mathias did. Safe in that I can talk to him and tell him how I feel. Safe, in that he somehow understands me.

After another sip of my brandy, I set the glass down and attempt to break the silence. "The thing is, that location is the only place in the area I can afford."

Nick sets his own glass down and startles me when he reaches for my arms and pulls me close to him to look me directly in the eyes. "Right now, I'm not sure if I should go beat the shit out of Bigelow for what he did to you or spank your ass until it turns red for still considering getting in bed with the devil."

Wide eyed, I swallow hard. But again, this is not fear. Not fear at all. I should be repulsed by his threat. I'm not. I'm actually somehow turned on by his chivalry. And how screwed up is that?

Obviously, I had read this situation completely wrong at the start of our conversation because it is clear Mathias Bigelow and Nick Carrington are anything but friends.

"I have a place I can show you tomorrow," he says.

The declaration throws me for a loop. "No, I don't think that's a good—"

Nick cuts me off before I can finish. "It's an old print shop that I've been saddled with for a while. The place needs a lot of work, and you'd be doing me a favor by taking it off of my hands. Besides, the rent is cheap."

As I stare into Nick's eyes, I consider his offer. I weigh the issues. The biggest being that this time I want to do this on my own. Because of this, I should say no. I probably shouldn't say yes. Yet, cheap is exactly what I need, and besides he wouldn't be involved.

I glance away, and then I quickly glance back. Words hover on the tip of my tongue, and finally I say them. "Okay, you can show me the property tomorrow, but no strings."

Nick gives me a nod. "No strings."

That nod that used to infuriate me is now making my pulse race.

What the hell?

With the touch of his fingertips searing through the fabric of my top, all I can think is—what is happening here?

I have no answer.

After he tells me a little bit about the rental space, I thank him and then stand to head to bed. He follows behind me. Upstairs, I turn to look at him before I enter my bedroom, and as I watch him close his door, I can't help but wonder what he and I are becoming.

Friends?

Not quite.

Business Associates?

Perhaps.

More?

Just maybe.

Ten

Nick

FOR THE PAST three and a half years I've referred to her as *Fiona's bitchy, stuck-up friend from New York City*. I don't even think I ever spoke of her by name.

Crazy enough, there are a million words swirling in my mind right now, but not a single one of them are any of those adjectives.

In fact, quite frankly, they seem rather ill-fitting to describe her at the present time.

And it's all because Tess Winters is standing beside me with a huge smile on her face. I honestly don't recall ever noticing how intoxicating her smile can be. Of course, it doesn't hurt that she looks hotter than fuck.

She's wearing tight jeans and a loose sweater. She's relaxed. Casual. Dare I say, bordering on fun. With her shoulder-length hair down, a knit cap on her head, and pure excitement in her brown eyes, she's practically gleaming as she takes in the large rental space.

I'm so fucking attracted to this side of her that I have to fight the urge to want to touch her—to press my palm to the small of her back, or brush my hand against hers, if only to watch the way her face flushes when I do. The blush is something she'd vehemently deny I'm sure, but it's there every time.

Every. Single. Time.

Since it's Saturday, Max doesn't have preschool. The original plan was for Tess to watch Max for the first half of the day and I'd take over around three. However, after my run I decided to blow off my late morning basketball game and take Tess to see the piece of property I told her about last night. I've been holding it for quite some time because the large square footage demands a steeper rent. Rent aside, my gut instinct tells me it just might be what Tess is looking for.

On the way to Printer's Row, I stopped at a park to let Max run around. With the amount of snow that has accumulated, the three of us were able to build a snowman. And a pretty good one at that. We also exchanged a snowball or two. I let Tess get a few my way. And yes, I did so because it made her smile.

"Uncle Nick. Uncle Nick. Uncle Nick." I glance down. Max is in his stroller, and eating some blueberries from a cup. He's pointing outside to the heavy falling snow.

Laughing, I rub his head. "Don't worry champ, we'll be outside again in a few minutes to see who can eat the most snowflakes."

Max giggles and so does Tess.

Unable to stop myself, I tease her with a slight bump to her shoulder. "You need to join in this time."

She shakes her head. "No way."

"Why? Are you too afraid you will look ridiculous?" I ask, and then open the door to the back room.

She steps in the large room and pivots around. "No, not at all. It looks fun. I'm just afraid my tongue will get frostbite."

My own tongue sneaks out to lick my lower lip, and then I talk before thinking. "If that happens, I know the perfect way to warm it up."

Tess gives me a curious look. "Are you flirting with me?"

Her directness puts me off balance, and my entire cool factor seems to fade away.

What the hell?

I have moves.

I know how to seduce women.

And yet every time I try with this girl she makes me feel weak in the knees. I have no idea why. All I know is I am done making a fool out of myself just to turn the situation around in my favor. This time, I'll be grown up about it. Saving face, I give her a look that says, "Don't be ridiculous," and then counter with, "I'm referring to drinking a cup of hot chocolate. My mind isn't always in the gutter."

"Right," she responds, and I swear she looks disappointed.

Moving past my ill-attempted obvious come on, I point to the far wall. "You could put a stove and an oven over there, a freezer too, and still have space for storage shelves."

She nods. "I was thinking the same thing."

I continue to layout the space; telling her where the electrical is and what could go where with the least amount of cost.

Just as I finish, she redirects her attention toward the front, as if there is a magnet pulling her in that direction. "The windows are just so amazing."

"Yeah, I agree. The entire storefront is glass, and perfect for a cafe."

The temperature in here is cold and Tess blows on her fingers. "I love that the people walking by will be able to see everything going on inside."

"It's definitely a plus."

She's practically bubbling with excitement. "The place has that old-fashioned feel to it. I'd love to be able to keep the charm of it. Who knows, maybe even someday find one of those antique cash registers."

"I think that's a great idea."

Tess reaches for her coat that I tossed with mine on an old rickety chair when we first entered the old space and takes her gloves from the pocket. "Just to be clear," she says, "the monthly lease amount you mentioned earlier is for this entire space?"

I give her a nod. "It is. Nothing has changed."

Sure, I might have chopped the rent a bit after she told me what happened with that prick, Mathias, but I had to get her away from him. That man has a bad reputation. I've met him a few times and truth be told, I can't stand him. Everyone knows he's connected, so crossing him isn't suggested. He's a shrewd businessman, a despicable guy, that's for sure, but his attitude when it comes to women is all about screwing them, in every sense of the word. And that isn't something I'd want anyone to be subject to.

"And the rent is fair?"

I nod, wondering if she's trying to chew me down.

"It seems way too low. I don't want any favors."

Okay, so getting me to lower the rent wasn't what she wanted. She's actually questioning if it's too low. Who does that? "Yes, it's fair," I answer. That isn't exactly true, but I know if I tell her the going rate, she'll walk and end up with Bigelow.

It's for her own good.

Slipping on her left glove, she pauses before putting on the other. "And no strings?"

Biting back a grin at her determination for independence, I shake my head. "No strings. The place is yours to do with what you want."

Tess squares her shoulders with pride.

"But," I add, "just to be clear, I can be a very helpful resource."

Instead of laughing, her lips part and the pink hint of her tongue appears when she delicately touches her top lip with it. "I bet you can."

Shoving the flirtation aside, I hope to make my point clear. "I'm serious, Tess. I know some of the best contractors in town. They won't rip you off or run away with your money."

She eyes me with suspicion. "And I won't owe you anything?"

It's abundantly obvious she's been burned, and most likely by that Frenchman of hers. "No, you won't owe me anything."

"Okay," she says.

"Okay," I grin.

With a bite of her lip, she extends her right arm. "I'll take it."

I take her proffered hand in mine and slowly shake it. The entire time my eyes are watching as the color of her cheeks flushes.

Yeah, I did that on purpose.

Quickly, she draws her hand back and covers it with her glove. "Thanks to you it looks like I won't have to get in bed with the devil."

There is so much in that statement I'd like to dissect.

The most hopeful line of thinking being . . . does she mean she'll get in bed with me instead?

Hey, I might have saved the day, but I never said I was a knight in shining armor.

Eleven

Tess

WITH CONSTRUCTION PAPER covering the table, and a couple pairs of blunt scissors lying on top of the messy piles, I stare out the picture window facing the street.

The weather hasn't improved at all. Snow is still falling, the temperature has dropped to near ten degrees, and ice is beginning to form everywhere.

With the roads in really bad condition, and visibility as poor as it is, it is very unlikely that many patrons will be out and about on this Sunday afternoon. Because of this, it is doubtful my planned scouting expedition to Printer's Row will give me the information I'm looking for, so I decide to postpone my research trip until tomorrow.

"Bye-bye," Max says, jarring me out of my thoughts.

I glance down at the phone screen.

Fiona looks so great—tanned and smiling. "Bye, my baby. Mommy loves you," Fiona says to Max, blowing him kisses.

"Daddy loves you too," Ethan adds, placing his hand on Fiona's bare thigh. The happy family moment makes my heart swell. Ethan comes closer, and it's then I notice that unfortunately he doesn't look tan like Fiona, but rather burned. Really, really painfully burned. Could it be karma perhaps? Okay that wasn't nice.

Rising to my feet, I take a step behind Max and wave at the two of them sitting happily on their hotel room bed. We've been facetime chatting for almost ten minutes, and I think Max has had his fill of remaining still.

As if on cue, Max looks back at me with his colored snowflake in his hand. "Can I go hang this one?" he asks in his cute toddler voice, where the words are sometimes hard to decipher.

I'm getting better at it at least.

Understanding most of his sentence, I offer him my hand to help him off the stool. "Yes, of course, but first say goodbye to Mommy and Daddy one more time."

"Bye," he calls as his little bare feet hit the floor and he trots over to the staircase where we are hanging our snowflake collection.

"I really miss him," Fiona says with a tear in her eye.

I snatch up the phone from where it is propped. "He misses you too."

"Are you sure he's doing okay?" Ethan asks, concern clear in his voice.

"He's more than okay," I reassure with a smile. "You have nothing to worry about, Nick and I are taking very good care of him."

"About that," Fiona winces, pulling the phone closer so it's only her and I visible on the screen.

I narrow my eyes at her. "Yes, about that." I haven't talked to Fiona since she left. We've texted, emailed, exchanged messages, but this is the first time we've been face to face.

"I should have called and warned you about Nick, I'm really sorry."

"Warned?" I hear Ethan sigh in the background. "It's not like he's trouble."

"That's not what I meant," Fiona clarifies. "You know they don't get along that well."

I decide not to say anything to Ethan because in my heart I know he did what he thought was best for Max. And to settle the issue there, I give Fiona a *don't worry about it* wave. I don't want her to feel bad. Besides, the situation is much better than I thought it would be. However, her and I will discuss this in private when she returns. "It's all good, honestly, Nick has been surprisingly very helpful."

"Speaking of Nick, is he around?" Ethan asks, taking the phone from Fiona.

"No, he left early this morning. He went to visit his brother at school."

"Can you tell him to call my office tomorrow about the new land deal in Miami?"

I shake my finger at him. "Tsk. Tsk. I thought you weren't working on your vacation?"

"I'm not. My paralegal just has a few quick questions for him. And Tess," he says.

"Yes," I reply.

"Thank you for everything."

This is about as close to an apology as I'll probably ever get from Ethan for springing Nick on me the way he did, so I accept it graciously. "You're welcome. Now stop arguing about the two of us and you two go have fun."

Fiona puts her head on Ethan's shoulder so I can see her. "Just remember, it wasn't me."

I shake my head.

Ethan turns to look at her. "Tess said that was enough."

"I know, but I want her to understand that—" Fiona tries to say.

Before she can finish, Ethan pushes his wife down on the mattress and she shrieks in surprise. I love the giggle I hear in her voice.

"Gotta go," she calls.

Shaking my head with a huge grin on my face, I hit the disconnect button because I'm not sure they are going to remember to.

My cell rings before I even set my phone down. I figure it's Fiona, but when I glance at the screen and see the name, I consider not answering it. He's called three times already, but I decide to pick it up this time. If not, I know he'll just call back.

"Hello," I answer.

"Miss Winters, it's Derrick Williams. How are you today?"

"I'm good."

"Great to hear. Listen, I was just wondering if you have signed Mr. Bigelow's lease yet? I could run over and pick it up."

I glance toward Max. "I'm sorry Derrick, but I won't be taking the property after all."

Derrick clears his throat. "Can I ask why not?"

"I found something better suited for my café, but thank you for your time."

"Yes, of course. Do you mind telling me what price you were quoted?"

I tell him. Not sure why he even cares. The deal is done.

"What should I tell Mr. Bigelow?" he asks.

"What I just told you, I suppose."

He clears his throat again. "May I ask where you found a more suitable location?"

"In Printer's Row."

Derrick is silent for a long while. "Thank you for your time, Miss Winters," he says and then hangs up.

That was strange.

Shrugging it off, I set my phone down and join Max to help him string the snowflakes. During the process he somehow manages to convince me he doesn't need to take a nap today.

It's almost three when Nick returns, our agreed upon time for the *change of shift*

"Hey," he says as he comes up the stairs.

He's wearing a ski jacket, beanie, and jeans, and my heart does a little pitter-patter when he comes into full view. I can't stop my reaction. He just looks so masculine. I promised myself I wouldn't compare Nick to Ansel, because come on, that is just stupid all the way around. And yet I find myself doing it. Whereas Nick is long and lean, toned and muscular, Ansel was thin. Fit, but thin. Whereas Nick fills out his clothes, Ansel's were never snug.

I run my tongue over my bottom lip.

I should stop.

But I don't.

Nick works out. Yes, he works out a lot. Ansel, on the other hand, refused to do anything but run. He said he was worried he'd get too bulky. Now I wonder if he was more worried he wouldn't. And yes, that puts a grin on my face.

Shoving the comparison aside and vowing never to do it again, I refocus on Nick. "Hey, what's all that?"

It's just now that I notice in his arms he is carrying a number of bags. "Groceries, just in case we end up getting snowed in," he remarks.

I leave Max to string the last of the cut pieces of paper around the bottom rail of the staircase banister and rush over to grab one of the bags from Nick. "God, I hope the storm doesn't get that bad. I have so much to do."

Nick sets the remaining bags in his arms down on the counter. "All the weather channels are predicting conditions will worsen overnight. You might have to postpone that to-do list of yours for a day or two."

I set the bag I'm holding down next to the others and sigh, knowing there is nothing I can do about the coming storm except stay inside to keep warm.

Nick begins to unpack the groceries, and I stand here, watching his muscular form as he moves around the kitchen.

When he hands me a can of coffee to put in the cabinet behind me, I catch a gleam in his blue eyes.

He's caught me staring again.

"Uncle Nick. Uncle Nick. Uncle Nick. Look!" Max shouts with excitement as he points to our snowflakes he has now successfully put on full display.

Nick grins over at Max, but I know he's smirking at me. "Wow, did you make all those?"

Feeling a blush coating my cheeks, I quickly look away from him and toward Max.

Max nods, pride evident in his eyes. "Auntie Tess and I did. Come see."

"In a minute, champ."

"I got this," I tell him, taking the boxes from his hands and being very careful to avoid coming in contact with his skin.

"You sure?" he asks, his eyes skimming down my body in a way I don't recall them ever doing.

I fight back a shiver. "Yes, go. Max has been waiting for you."

His gaze sharpens when it climbs back up and reaches my eyes. "Yeah, I bet he has. I promised him I'd take him outside to build a fort when I got back, but I don't think it's a good idea."

I try to remain calm, but something inside me feels on fire. "No, I don't think so either. I told him it might be too cold. That's why we started making it snow inside."

Nick strides away with a grin I can't quite place. He seems to take his time as he removes his outerwear. Just before he reaches Max, he glances over his shoulder, and it's then I figure out what he is doing. He's watching me watch him.

I quickly look away.

"Burrrr . . . it's really cold in here. Are those real?" he says to Max.

At the sound of his voice, I turn back. I can't help myself. I watch a little longer. And I can't help but smile when I see the excitement in Max's eyes that Nick has returned. Max shows Nick the snowflakes and Nick admires each one.

Sucking in a huge breath, I blow it out and get to work putting the rest of the food away.

Since I've already decided to stay home, I offer to cook stir-fry for dinner. Even though cooking has never been my thing, I did pick up a few things at culinary school, so there are a few dishes I can cook fairly well, stir-fry being one of those meals.

Nick, still busy examining each piece of paper, quickly takes me up on my offer.

It's not long before he and Max have moved on. Now they are getting to serious work building a fort inside with pillows and blankets.

Turning the music on low and grabbing a glass of wine, I get to work cleaning the vegetables I will need for dinner. Once done, I decide to go ahead and prep them as well. After all, the boys are buried deep under mounds of blankets, so I have time to myself. With that, I grab a knife and start slicing carrots on the chopping board. I can't help but pray I won't end up cutting my thumbs into flesh-colored matchsticks. After all, it's been a long while since I've done this.

Lost in my thoughts as I'm chopping away, a hand on my shoulder and a voice in my ear startles me. "I usually cut them into chunks," Nick says.

His voice is thick and husky and my nipples tighten from the sound. I have this strange urge to lean back against him, press my back to his front, feel his hardness, sway to the music. But the thoughts are ludicrous. Instead of falling into my crazy, I stand a little straighter and say to Nick, "All vegetables need to be as thin as possible for them to cook properly."

He's already at the refrigerator before I even finish speaking, and my fantasy of him kissing my neck with his strong hands tight on my hips is instantly crushed as soon as he opens it and grabs a beer. "So that's the secret," he smirks, popping off the top, "And here I thought it never came out right because of my cooking."

Grabbing for the onion, I stab the white skin with the tip of the knife and kick myself for hoping he came in here to see me. "That could be it too," I joke, wanting to keep the banter going to mask my disappointment.

Nick points his bottle my way. "Watch it, cocky has consequences."

"Maybe I like consequences."

Okay, so I'm flirting back even though I told myself I wouldn't. Told myself that Nick Carrington is a world-class flirt. I mean come on; I've seen him in action many times. And yet, I'm doing just that. And to boot, it seems I can't help myself.

"Uncle Nick, Uncle Nick, Uncle Nick." Max has entered the kitchen. His little voice carries a bit of annoyance in it that makes me laugh. "You said you were just going to check on Tess and come right back."

So Nick did come in here to see me.

The very thought makes me giddy.

Nick says nothing in response to Max's complaint. He just sets his bottle down, scoops Max up and places him on his shoulders, and then gallops into the living room. "Come on, we have some things to discuss in the fort," he tells Max as he sets him down.

"What kind of things?" Max asks in his cute voice.

"Manly things," Nick responds.

"Manly? What's that?"

"I'm about to explain it to you," Nick whispers before covering them both up and turning on the flashlight.

At that, I take another sip of my wine and try not to laugh out loud because seriously, this situation is laughable. I'm co-sitting with a man I thought I hated, and turns out, I might kind of like him. And he might just kind of like me too. And how dumb is that—at my age, I certainly know better than to fall for the likes of Nick Carrington.

I really do.

Twelve

Tess

MEAL PREPPING IS tedious business—popcorn is so much easier.

Twenty minutes later, I have finally finished. Now I feel like my entire body smells of onions, peppers, and broccoli. Hating the vegetable smell on my skin, I decide since I haven't showered yet today that I have time to take a quick one before I start dinner.

Without a word, I slip away.

Upstairs, I'm faced with a tough decision—shower or bath. The bathroom off of Fiona and Ethan's room is old and only has a bathtub with a shower sprayer, which means you have to stand and hold the sprayer over you.

Not very relaxing.

The only other full bathroom is all the way down on the bottom floor, and Nick has been using that one. Fiona and Ethan plan to remodel their bathroom to add a shower, but they haven't gotten to that renovation yet.

Not wanting to invade on the space I practically ordered Nick to take, I opt for the tub. Turning on the warm water, I run the bath and add some of Fiona's lavender oil to it. Soon enough I'm settling in. I let the water enfold me, hold me, cradle me even as I sink deeper and deeper.

When the water is at the halfway level, I let my chin rest on the surface and start thinking about this past week.

Nick is so different from what I thought he was. I thought he was a jerk, so I never bothered to look any further. Now, I'm not only looking, I'm seeing way more than I should be. Feeling way more than I should be. Wanting way more than I should be.

Want.

Need.

Desire.

I'm feeling it all.

So much so that I find myself sliding my hands down my body in the hot water. The bath oil makes my skin slick. Smooth. Soft. Slippery enough that my palms skid over my stomach and thighs with ease.

Because I haven't had sex or even masturbated in months, my arousal seems heightened. Desperate even.

Sinking lower into the deep tub, with my ears now in the water, I'm able to hear the wildly beating thump of my heart.

The pitter-patter caused by thoughts of him.

Thoughts I shouldn't be having.

And despite this, I am spurred on by the sound of my own heart. Without a second thought, I cup my breasts. Stroke them. Pass my palms over my nipples before pinching them both between my fingers. A sigh leaks out of me as they burn and tighten.

His voice is in my head. "Cocky has consequences."

Consequences.

I want them, and I don't even know what they are.

I tug and tug and tug until I feel an answering pull in my clit. I move the firm flesh back and forth, tugging on them harder and harder, waiting for it to feel like his hands are on me.

I want to know what that feels like—in the worst way.

Needing more, I open my legs and push my hips against the water. Still tugging on one of my nipples, I slide my other hand down between my thighs.

My clit is more than ready for my touch, *his* touch.

I bite my lip, the gentle stroke enough to make my hips jerk toward the surface. Still it's not enough. Not nearly enough. *Not him.*

Needing even more, I apply pressure and circle my clit. The water supports me and lifts me, but not for long. Soon I'm pushing my pelvis against my fingers and my shoulder blades bump the bottom of the tub.

His hands.

His big, callused palms.

Rough and soft.

His long, strong fingers.

That's what I want to feel.

That's what I pretend I feel.

Sliding two fingers inside, I try to make believe it is okay I'm daydreaming about *him.* And for a minute, it is okay.

It's only pretend.

I think of him and the way he moves, and my clit swells, opening my body with an ache that needs to be filled.

By him.

By his huge cock.

By the time I realize I shouldn't be thinking this way about him, it's too late. I can't stop. I imagine it's *him* in here with me. Not my own fingers. And he is fucking me. Fucking me hard in the alpha way he has about him. Telling me to sit on his lap. To ride his hard cock. And I do. I do just as he says. Soon, we're all tongues and hands, and fucking like animals. With an image in my mind that can never take place in the real world, I explode in a small whirlwind of lust.

It's an orgasm that rocks me.

Makes me feel alive for the first time in months.

I may not know what it is about Nick Carrington that is making me feel like I want to get close to him and keep my distance at the same time, but I do know for absolute certainty that I needed this. Needed this to put an end to the craziness going on in my head about a man I certainly don't need to get involved with.

About a man who's pure temptation.

About a man who I know can only bring me heartache.

"Stop," I order myself.

And I think I can now. I tell myself that I will get out of here and put those animalistic desires to rest as soon as I do.

Stepping out of the claw foot tub is tricky. I didn't plan very well. The floor is wet and the towels are across the room.

Just as I take my first step the door bursts open. "Auntie Tess. Auntie Tess. Auntie Tess. We're going to have a campout. Uncle Nick started a fire. Come see, come see."

The doorknob is broken, and therefore the door could not be locked. I'd completely forgotten about that, but it's just Max, and I although I want to hurry to grab a towel, I'm afraid I'll slip and fall, so I step carefully, but swiftly. "That sounds like so much fun. I'll be down as soon as I get dressed," I tell him softly.

"Max," Nick yells coming to an instant stop in the doorway.

Now I'm like a deer in the headlights. I have no idea what to cover first. My breasts? My sex? Like one of those dumb movies, I place one arm across my small breasts, the other going down allowing my hand to shield my sex.

Nick's gaze simmers over me for the longest time, and then a smile curves his lips. "Ummm . . . sorry about this. I tried to stop him from coming up, but he was too excited about the campout. I had no idea you were bathing."

My eyes widen. I consider waving him away, but I'll expose myself even more if I use my hands. I consider yelling for him to go already, but that will scare Max. So I do neither. Instead I remain calm. I saw him naked. Now he saw me. No big deal. Right? "Yes, I thought I'd clean up before dinner. How about you two boys go downstairs and finish setting up?" I suggest.

Nick seems to be enjoying himself. Staring at me. At what he can see, which isn't much.

"Nick," I prod.

He scratches his messy hair, shifts his eyes back and forth, and then absently says, "Yeah, Max, come on buddy, Tess could use from privacy."

"Privacy?" Max asks, "What's that?"

Nick's gaze is practically sizzling now as his eyes travel over me. "Well, it's when someone, well . . ." As Nick struggles to try to explain the word to Max, he takes his hand and leads him away, leaving the door open behind him, and looking back one last time before disappearing out of the bedroom.

Temptation is clear in his gaze, as I'm sure it must be in mine. And just like that, my little pep talk seems irrelevant.

It's now very apparent—we are both in so much trouble.

Thirteen

Nick

ETHAN IS A cheap bastard.

It's true.

Fact in point, I have repeatedly offered to personally assist him with the renovations of his old house, and yet he keeps saying no. He says he has a budget. A plan. A schedule.

Did I mention a budget?

Since he hates to spend money, he hasn't been in a huge hurry to update or fix anything. And after more than three years, the majority of repairs are still left undone. Of course the one thing he did take care of is converting the old gas heater to a new electric one.

Go figure.

The power had been flickering on and off before going out completely thirty minutes ago, and leaving this old house with a brutal chill.

Thank fuck the wood-burning fireplace is roaring in front of the three of us, and keeping us warm. It's eight o'clock at night and Max is out cold.

When Max and I decided to have a campout, I had set up three piles of blankets and pillows in the shape of a triangle, so no one was stuck in the middle. Max's words, not mine. Anyway, it's a good thing I set up camp because it looks like until the power goes back on, we'll all be sleeping here on the living room floor.

Lying back on the pillow with my hands behind my head, I glance down to see Tess's messy bun moving on top of her head. The same way she was wearing her hair when I saw her naked mere hours ago. Something I wouldn't mind seeing again, sometime very soon by the way. "You awake?" I whisper.

She twists onto her side to look up at me. "I am."

My voice is low. "Listen. I want you to know I'm sorry about earlier. I honestly had no idea you were taking a bath."

The flush on her cheeks could be from the fire, but I highly doubt it. "It's not a big deal. I saw you naked, now you've seen me."

Trying not to remember how turned on I was by the sight of her and her beautiful backside that I know I shouldn't have been staring at in the mirror, I make light of her comment. "Yeah, I guess that makes us even."

She laughs that soft laugh that does something to my gut I can't explain. "Well, not quite."

Speechless, I give her a quizzical look wondering if she busted me for the sideways glances in the mirror when I thought I was being so sly.

"Don't you remember?" she asks, "You mooned me at Ethan and Fiona's barbeque last year."

Okay, time to fess up. "About that. I know you think I was mooning you because I heard you call me a jerk, but it honestly had nothing to do with you."

"Right," she scuffs.

"It wasn't you I was mooning. I swear."

Confusion clouds her features.

"It's true. You just happened to walk outside right after Jace dared me to flash your Andy."

Tess flops onto her stomach and rises on her elbows. Her oversized button-down shirt gapes open and I wonder if it belonged to him. The thought provokes the oddest feeling of jealousy in me.

"You know his name is Ansel," she remarks with a sigh, "and I told you, he's not mine anymore. But all that aside, why would Jace dare you to do that?"

With my neck straining to look at her, and the top swells of her tiny breasts all I can see, I decide to avoid temptation and reposition myself. Moving beside her, facing the same direction as she is, I prop myself up on one elbow and look into her brown eyes. "Truth?"

She mimics my pose and stares back. "Always."

"Jace was drunk and he swore the dude had a thing for me. He wanted me to test it out."

Tess moves the palm that was resting on her outer thigh to the open neck of her shirt, and says, "Wait. What? Why would you think that?"

"Who knows? It was dumb. We were drunk and just being stupid."

"Ansel might have had a wandering eye, but I can assure you it was for women only."

My body tenses from the hurt I see in her eyes. "Did he cheat on you? Is that why you two broke up?"

She nods. Sadness seems to grip her and I can tell she knows it shows on her face when she sucks in a deep breath.

"I shouldn't have asked. It's not my business."

I'm surprised when she plunges forward. "It's okay. Yes, that's what happened. He cheated on me."

"I'm sorry. Do you want to talk about it?"

"There's not much to say. I caught him one night in the kitchen of our restaurant with a liquor sales rep after hours. Once I opened my eyes, I discovered he'd been screwing other women right under my nose for years. Probably the entire time we were together."

A low growl escapes my throat because I want to fucking kill him. This girl is honest, smart, sexy, funny—the whole package, and that douchebag has the nerve to treat her like shit. What a goddamned asshole.

"At first I felt like a fool. I mean, I should have known. Right?"

I shrug. "Not if you weren't looking."

Her laugh is bitter. "That's just it, I wasn't. I was working. I thought he was too. We were trying to make the restaurant a success. I never thought to worry about someone else. I honestly believed what we had was enough for him."

I clench my hand into a fist, trying to fight the anger I feel for the dick that hurt Tess. "It should have been."

Tess dives into more detail, telling me about how her and Ansel met right after her parents died. That she was vulnerable and alone, and he was there. It was what she needed at the time. Once she tells me about the ups and downs of their long-term relationship, she returns to their breakup. "At first, he tried to convince me that his predilection for other women was poor judgment on his part, and that he was sorry. That what we had was enough. He actually wanted me to give him another chance."

"Fucker," I mutter.

She smiles but it doesn't show in her eyes. "Right. I mean he was my boyfriend and he was supposed to love me. What he had been doing wasn't love."

"What did you tell him?" I ask.

"What else could I say other than we were over? Even if my feelings for him hadn't changed, I could never trust him again."

I push a stray piece of hair from her eyes. "Good for you."

She sighs unhappily. "Well, not really. I not only lost him, but the restaurant too. So look where my trust issues got me?"

I glance around and grin. "It got you back to Chicago, and here, with me. That isn't so bad."

This time she laughs a real laugh. "What about you?"

"What about me?"

"Have you ever had a girlfriend?"

"Not really."

"Why not?"

It takes a few moments to decide how to answer her, but then I decide to tell Tess the truth—to tell her all about my mother. How the woman had grown up in Las Vegas, was on her own since she was sixteen, married some guy at seventeen, but divorced him soon after for reasons she never told my father. She then moved to Chicago and met my father. Out of the blue, some twelve years later, a guy claiming to be her ex-husband shows up at our doorstep and the next day she disappears from our life, never to return. We haven't heard from her since, then again, we never went looking. After twenty minutes I think I've told her more about myself than I've told anyone at one time—ever.

Tess lays her head on her pillow and tugs her blanket up a little higher. "Nick, I'm really sorry that happened to you, but you can't put a wall around yourself because of it."

With a yawn, I lay my own head on my pillow. "I didn't build a wall around myself," I reassure her before closing my eyes.

It went up all by itself.

Fourteen

Tess

THERE'S A NOISE, and I awake with a start.

For a moment I feel disorientated and it takes a minute to gain my bearings. I can't immediately place my surroundings. Then, as my eyelids flutter open, I see Nick lowering himself, squatting down beside me. His sleepy blue eyes are watching me with intensity.

Alarmed, I sit up and look around the dimly lit room. "Where's Max?"

Nick places his hand on my shoulder to calm me. "The power is back on and I just brought him upstairs to his bed."

Okay, the creaky staircase is the noise I heard. Relieved, I flop back down, not ready to move. "What time is it?" I ask groggily.

"Almost six."

I groan. "In the morning?"

"In the morning," he reassures me, offering me his hand. "Come on, I'll help you off the floor. It's time to get up anyway."

Declining, I roll to my side and peek up at Nick through my lashes. "God, it feels like I never went to sleep."

"That's because it was almost two before you stopped talking."

To shield the lights from the kitchen, I tug the blanket up over my head. "That's so not true. You were the one doing all the talking."

"Whatever," he says. "I'm going to go for a run. Do you want a hand getting up or not?"

Lowering the covers, I sit up and look out the window at the still heavily falling snow. "You're going outside in this weather? Are you nuts? I think I'll stay right here where it's warm."

Nick laughs and flops down beside me on his back. "You have a point. I think I'll hit the treadmill at my office later today."

I laugh too, and groan a little when I shift in my pile of blankets from the lack of comfort that comes from lying on the floor. "Wow, you have a treadmill at your office?"

"Not just a treadmill, an entire gym. Come by later if you want and workout."

I laugh again. "I haven't worked out in months. I'm not sure I remember how."

"Then you really should come by. I could give you a pointer or two to help you get back on track."

My eyes dart to the spot where his long-sleeve t-shirt has lifted, and then my gaze slowly slides up his hard body until it lands on his face. "Right. So I can make a fool of myself," I respond, hearty laughter still in my voice. "I think I'll pass, thank you very much."

Nick's staring at me again with that same intensity I saw when I first woke up. This time though, his breathing is hitched, and I can't help but wonder if he's thinking the same thing I am.

Still laughing, I fall onto my back and keep my focus on him.

"God, you have a beautiful laugh," he says hoarsely.

My entire body reacts to the look he's giving me, and all I can do is keep staring. I have no words, no smartass comeback, nothing.

Moments pass where all we share is a look. It's a look that screams, *"I want you, do you want me?"*

Slowly, Nick nods his head.

At the same time, I nod mine.

And then Nick is rolling, shifting his body, and in a beat he's above me looking down into my eyes. Within moments, his body is covering mine with the twisted blankets around his hips. He maneuvers himself until my thighs are spread and I can feel his heavy erection through the fabric of his track pants right between my legs.

"I want you," he rasps, grinding his hips into mine in the most delicious way.

"I want you too," I respond breathlessly, lifting my pelvis to meet his slow and distinct movements.

He pushes some stray pieces of hair from my eyes. "Are you sure about this?" he whispers.

"I'm sure," I whisper back.

Without another word, Nick quickly gets to his feet. The fire is still roaring. Nick must have stoked it when he woke, and I suddenly feel extremely warm.

With my heart pounding, I watch him as he strides toward the kitchen. Watch his long lean body, watch the confidence in his walk, watch the pure male who might have decided against this very poor decision we both made days ago but are just now acting on. But then he picks up his wallet and pulls out a condom. When he strides back in my direction, there is purpose intent on his face. And my heart pounds even more.

Standing above me with his brilliant blue eyes on me, he drops the condom to the ground and pulls his t-shirt off. I stare at his ripped abs, biting my lip, wanting to taste him so bad I can hardly stand it.

There is no hesitation in my next move. With my gaze locked on him, I sit up and slowly unbutton my own shirt in spite of my trembling fingers. He watches me, his chest rising and falling even faster than moments ago. Once I shrug out of the oversized shirt, my small breasts are completely exposed to him.

Nick sucks in a breath. "God, you're so fucking beautiful. I can't wait to be inside you."

I can't wait either. I want this. And right now. So, I pull my leggings off, panties too, and sit naked in front of the fire. In front of him.

If Nick is surprised by my forwardness, he doesn't show it. Instead, he strips out of his own pants and then finally lowers himself down to me.

He takes his time putting himself back in the position he had been in before he went to retrieve a condom. It's slow, torturous, and amazing. His breath whispers across my neck. His skin feels so good against my own. And his body is like it was made for mine. Once he is pressing firmly against me, he presses his lips to mine.

Our first kiss is with the both of us completely naked. Completely open to each other. Vulnerable. And both more than ready to be together.

His lips move soft, then hard, against mine, and then he pushes his tongue into my mouth. Soon our tongues begin to move together, and his kiss consumes me.

My hands slide down his back to his firm ass and I pull him against me. "I want you inside me, now."

I thought he'd fight me. Tell me he was in control. Show that alpha male dominance I have seen so many times. He does none of those things. Instead, Nick reaches with one hand and retrieves the condom he'd tossed beside me. My pulse races with an odd excitement, one I never recall having prior to intercourse. I watch him tear away the wrapper with his teeth and sheath himself with the latex, and I'm completely overtaken by lust.

It all starts to happen very quickly after that. He is obviously just as desperate as me for this. His fingers slide inside me, and as soon as he feels how wet I am, he shudders. Within seconds, his fingers are gone and he slides his cock into me. It's with his first thrust that I realize I was wrong—he is the one in control, this is what he wanted too, and all I can do is gasp because he feels so good.

Moments after he starts to thrust, he pauses in his movements. He's still staring down at me, but this time his eyes are tender in a way I've never seen them. "I've wanted you from the first time I saw you at Ethan and Fiona's engagement party. Everything I've done and said to you since that night has been to fight the need to have you."

I open my mouth to speak, unsure of what to say.

He prevents me from saying anything with a heart-stopping kiss, and around the kiss he says, "Don't say anything."

I don't.

Nick starts to move again, pulling back and easing forward, pushing gently until he is all the way inside me again.

Almost instinctively, I reach up, wrapping my arms around his neck, and holding onto him tightly.

Our bodies tangle and clash, twisting and rolling until I am breathless and panting. Nick groans low in his throat and again he surprises me when he pushes his arms underneath me so he can hold me closer against his body.

He's fucking me hard and fast, and making love to me soft and slow, all at the same time. I've thought about little more than this for days, but never had I imagined it to be this good.

Nick's hips arch fluidly, his cock slides in and out of my body until I am practically dizzy with pleasure.

His body is pressed so hard against mine that I can feel every twitch, feel every time his muscles coil and bunch with the effort of his movements, feel every ounce of energy he expels.

In fact, we are so close I don't think there is a part of me he isn't touching in some way. It's like he can't get enough of me, and the thought sends a shiver racing down my spine.

It hits me when he tears his mouth from mine to press a line of kisses down my jaw to my neck that I thought sex with Nick would be quick, dirty, and emotionally bereft.

This is anything but.

Suddenly, I'm overwhelmed by my feelings, and I'm climbing that endless mountain of pleasure even faster.

Nick is surrounding me, touching me, filling me, filling me in places that have been hollow and aching for way longer than three months.

Soon I find myself hugging him to me. Like him, I can't stand for the barest of inches to separate us. When I am close to reaching the top of the mountain, I cling to him so tightly, I'm sure I will leave marks. It's then that my body starts to shake with an uncertainty as to what this is and why it is happening.

Perhaps feeling I'm close, or perhaps close himself, Nick rocks into me, deeper, harder, faster.

Still uncertain as to what is happening, why there is such a profound connection between the two of us, I close my eyes.

"Tess." Nick's tender voice pulls me from my scattered thoughts. "Look at me."

I open my eyes to see him staring intently down at me.

"Are you okay?"

I nod.

"You sure?"

Again I nod, and this time I hug him tighter. "Kiss me."

He does. Fiercely.

I shiver and arch my body.

"How close are you?" he whispers.

"Almost there," I whisper back.

"Tell me what you need to get there?"

What I need? I've never been asked that, and I answer with the one word my body is telling me will send me over the edge. "You."

His eyes flash and his jaw clenches. Then he is kissing me again. Harder. Hot. Nipping. Licking. Sucking. Until I am breathing his air and he is breathing mine.

We are locked together so tightly that I have no idea how he manages to keep thrusting. With each movement he makes, my release is building low and deep. So deep, I feel like I'm being turned inside out. "Oh, God," I moan. And then I'm on the top of that mountain and for a moment I'm afraid to fall. Afraid of what will happen when it's all over, but it's too late, and before I can stop myself, I'm coming around his cock.

"Fuck," Nick groans as he begins to move faster, harder. Any control he had is gone and he's pushing into me so deep that I gasp at his depth.

That's when I begin to unravel. I thought I'd come just seconds ago, but now my orgasm is owning me, taking me over, making me slick and wet, and out of control.

I squeeze him tightly, never wanting this feeling to end. Gasping his name, I close my eyes and the world blurs around me. All I can feel is him. On top of me. His mouth on my skin. His cock buried deep. The noises he is making. Him. All of him. All around me.

When I start to float downward, my body feels weightless, sated, free. It's a strange new feeling. I can't quite grasp it.

I'm not sure I want to.

Nick collapses on top of me. His body is limp and his chest heaves with exertion, but he feels so good, and I want him to stay right where he is.

I press my lips to his neck and start to suck.

Nick laughs, and rolls so that I'm on top of him. "You, Tess Winters, are incredible."

I look down at him. "You aren't so bad yourself."

"You mean for a jerk," he jokes.

I narrow my eyes at him. "Stop with that, please."

He smiles and kisses me softly. "Since you said please."

This time I roll my eyes.

He kisses me again, this time harder. "Let me get rid of the condom and then I want to do that again, but this time I want to taste you first."

With my legs still shaking and my body still trembling, I roll onto my back. "We have at least another hour before Max wakes, so if you insist."

Nick cocks a brow and then makes his way upstairs. Within seconds he is back beside me, reaching for me and tugging me on top of him. "I want to say that was unexpected, but that would be a lie. After the last five days it wasn't," he laughs.

"No, it wasn't," I laugh back.

His fingertips trail down my back and my body responds in the same way it has since the first time he touched me. "Are you sure you didn't want me from the first time you saw me?"

I rise to my elbows, my fingers going to his hair and threading through it. "After what we just did, I want to say yes, but that would be a lie."

"Way to hurt a guy's ego," he responds with color in his voice.

Twisting my lips, I stare down into his blue eyes. "I doubt that ego of yours has ever even been scratched."

Nick slaps my bare bottom and rolls me onto my back, spreading my legs wide as he hovers between them. "Shut up and let me taste you."

And for once, I have no problem doing just as he says.

Fifteen

Tess

SEX CHANGES EVERYTHING.

No matter how many times you say it won't, or want to pretend things will be the same afterwards, they won't be.

They never are.

For Nick and I, that isn't saying much. After three years of war, the cease-fire had resulted in both of us crying out each other's names, and now trying to catch our breath.

It isn't anything I would have predicted.

My breasts are crushed against his chest when I spot the sun rising. "We should probably get dressed," I say, "Max will be waking up soon."

His muscles grow taut beneath me, and with an uneasy feeling stirring in my belly that I can't shake, I wait for it.

This was a mistake.

This shouldn't have happened.

This is a one-time thing

Or better yet—don't get too attached to me.

"Yeah, you're right," Nick says, sitting up and forcing me to do the same.

He runs a hand through his hair, and then looks around before standing. As he gathers my clothes and hands them to me, I wait for it. Nothing. I start to wonder just how bad this is going to be.

We still have nine days together; will we be able to do it?

Time to find out.

"Nick," I call as I shrug into my shirt.

He turns, just finishing pulling his pants up. God, that body. It's hard not to stare at it. "Yeah," he says, his voice thick.

That's when I do something very unlike me, and go fishing. "We probably shouldn't have done that."

Standing there shirtless, he puts his hands on his hips and raises a brow. "Look Tess, I'm not going to play games. If you're looking for me to agree because you think you know me so well, I'm not going. Or if you're waiting for me to tell you it was a mistake, that's not going to happen either."

Honestly, can he just address the statement? Agitated, I can't help but shake my head, because really, he can be such a jerk. "Alright then," I say, and get to my feet, my body language sending out all kinds of vibes. What vibes though, I can't even be clear.

Whatever he reads them as, it's not anger or hostility I can tell you that because his eyes greedily take me in.

I smirk at the heat I see in them, but then quickly remember I'm put off by his attitude and turn away to gather the pillows. Still, I can't help but steal a glance or two his way.

He's poking at the fire when he looks over his shoulder and catches my gaze. "Do you really think that?"

I'm just about to set the pillows on the couch when I freeze. I could lie and tell him yes, or I could be honest. In the end, I decide to be honest. As soon as I finish my task, I whirl around. "No, but I thought you might, so I wanted to make it easier for you."

Nick is a lot of things, but gracious and humble aren't any of them. With amusement glittering in his eyes, he says, "Awww . . . that's really sweet Tess, you were worried about me."

Now I'm infuriated. "Screw you," I say with more force than I intended. "I just didn't want things to feel awkward between us."

He throws his head back and laughs. Laughs. The nerve of him. When he settles himself, he sets those eyes on me. "Oh, and if I had said thanks for the lay, but don't get to attached to me, that wouldn't have been awkward?"

I stare at him. "Why are you being such a jerk about this?"

Nick sets the poker down and strides toward me with a predatory light in his eyes I've never seen before. My heart slams right out of my chest. When he stops in front of me, he gently wraps his fingers around my upper arms and says, "You're the one who made the comment. Perhaps you should just apologize to me for thinking so little of me, and then we can plan our day. It looks like neither of us will be going to work, and obviously school will be canceled, so let's make the most of it."

My jaw drops open. "You want me to apologize to you?"

He nods, and simply says, "Yes, and then we can plan our day, together."

I'm a little torn here. On one hand, wow, I was so not expecting that, on the other hand, is he really serious? I decided on the latter. "You're unbelievable," I say, and turn to march up the stairs.

He catches me before I reach the first step, and I whirl around. "If you're worried this was a one-night stand for me, it wasn't," he says in a low voice, no more menacing in his tone.

There is nothing but the truth in his eyes.

"I just thought you should know," he adds.

I swallow, and blow out a slow exhale. "Thank you," I say, and then tack on, "And I am sorry. I was fishing."

Nick steps up, and forces me back. I end up sitting on one of the steps, looking up at him. He runs his hands possessively up my arms, over my shoulders, along my throat, and then he cradles my face, where he proceeds to crush his lips to mine. He kisses me like he's starved. Like I'm the only thing that matters. *Like I'm his.*

Hot.

Torrid.

Consuming.

His breath explodes over me as he breaks contact with my lips, and we both gasp for air, and then he says, "Now, Tess, is that settled?"

My body is quivering from head to toe as I look up at him, and then I do the only thing I can, and nod.

With Nick, you just never know what to expect . . .

Except the unexpected.

Sixteen

Nick

SNOW DAYS COULD be compared to hitting the jackpot—when I was a kid that is.

As an adult, usually I see them as a giant pain in the ass. With schools closed, businesses closed, and roads closed, conducting work as normal is just a wet dream. Today though, I find myself saying—I fucking love snow days.

The Rover can get through anything, but by noon it's completely unnecessary to engage the four-wheel drive. The snow has stopped and the sun is out. Instead of going to the office though, I decide to take Tess and Max out for the day. We all dress warm and go skating at Warren Park Ice Rink. There I get to show off my skills on the ice. Having played hockey most of my life, I can honestly say I know how to skate. Tess isn't so bad herself. And Max is having a blast wearing blades for the first time.

After that we make our way to Cloud Gate. I haven't stopped by the giant bean in years. Neither has Tess. In front of the giant silver sculpture, Tess takes a million pictures of Max and texts them to

Fiona and Ethan. She also insists I take a selfie, of which I refuse. Somehow she manages to wear me down and I end up snapping one just to shut her up. She's relentless when she wants something.

We then make our way to Mindy's Hot Chocolate to warm up. Max has two cups, and Tess has one. I settle on coffee, but Max makes me taste his hot chocolate because it is the best ever with so many extra marshmallows.

We spend the later part of the afternoon driving around Printer's Row. There I give Tess a tour of the whats and wheres. Once I've showed her around, I take her and Max into my office just to check on things, after which we hit the drive-thru at McDonalds to feed Max because he pleaded. And then we make one last stop at a local Italian restaurant for the adults.

By the time we get home it's after seven and Max is out cold. Carrying him up the stairs has become a habit, but I don't mind. The little guy has so much energy that his body just can't keep up.

In his room, I lay him down at the foot of the bed.

"I guess I'll bathe Max tomorrow," Tess says as she pulls off his shoes and then tugs down the bedcovers.

I pick him up again and carry him to the head of the bed. "Shit, I forgot about that. Don't tell Fi we put him to bed without a bath, she'll freak."

Tess laughs as she turns on his nightlight. "That secret is safe with me. Fiona is a little crazy about baths, and I think she'd have my head for putting him to bed without one."

I raise a brow. "You could have my head."

Tess shoves me toward the door. "Out," she orders.

In the hall, I lean against the spare room door with one foot propped up and wait for Tess to finish tucking Max in.

Today has been filled with illicit touches and covert looks. I don't think I've ever felt this much sexual tension without satisfying it. So yeah, right now the word head makes me think of my throbbing cock. Just like watching her bend down earlier made me think of her sweet pussy. And seeing her pucker her lips around her cup of hot chocolate created visions of how that mouth would feel wrapped around me.

Tess comes out of the room, closes the door, and then turns to look at me across the hall. "We should eat while the food is hot."

I shrug. "We could always warm it up."

She eyes the door I'm leaning against, the one to the spare room. "Ask me nicely."

I remain right where I am. "Ask you what?"

"If I want to fuck?"

Amused, I go ahead and ask, "Do you want to fuck?"

She shrugs. "I am hungry. Maybe if you ask a little nicer."

"What? Do you want me to beg?"

Her eyes light up. "That just might satisfy my hunger for now."

I raise a brow. "I don't beg."

She doesn't move, or say anything.

We're at a draw.

Let's see if she's feeling the same urgency that I am.

"Okay, let's eat," I say, and slowly step for the stairs.

Within seconds she grabs me by the collar of my shirt and tugs me inside the spare room.

I let her.

Once inside, I kick the door closed.

Then she tugs my shirt off and pushes me against the wall.

Starving for a taste of her, I yank her sweater off and then rip her blouse open to see those tiny pink nipples, to pinch them, lathe them with my tongue. Before I can remove her bra and close my mouth around one of them though, she drops to her knees in front of me.

Holy fuck.

Without fumbling, she yanks my belt open, undoes my button, and unzips my zipper. My straining cock pushes at the front of my boxers and I'm in her fist before I even have a chance to make a sound.

Tess uses one knee to nudge my legs farther apart as she pulls my pants down to my thighs. My boxers, too. I'm mostly naked for her in half a minute.

My cock pulses against her palm as she skims her hand upward, barely brushing my head, but enough that my hips jerk forward in excitement. As soon as they do, she grips my shaft, keeping me in place.

Oh, fuck.

I flatten my palms against the wall and hold on. I have never been at a woman's mercy like this. Sure, I've been blown a million times, but never when I wasn't the one in control. And never have I wanted to be out of control as much as I do right now.

I look down at her, my gaze darkening with an unbelievable bout of lust. Her gaze drifts up, and I see in it the same.

And in that single moment that our eyes lock, she opens her mouth and let's her hot breath seep over my even hotter flesh.

It makes me shiver.

With a smile on her face, she brushes my cock against her cheek, close, so close, and yet my tip is not quite close enough to be inside her mouth.

Lower.

Lower.

A little lower.

Not low enough.

Shit.

Teasing me, she breathes against my cock as her hand works it. And then she turns her head, mouthing the inside of my thigh, nuzzling it, and then she nips it and I cry out. I want to reach down and push her head so her mouth is right there, right on my cock, but I don't.

I'm giving her this.

Letting her control this.

When she runs her tongue along the underside of my cock, stopping just before she reaches the tip, I close my eyes and let my head drop. The long, tortured cry that escapes my throat isn't a sound I've ever made.

Oh, fuck, she's using her teeth and my body is shaking in a way I am powerless to stop.

Soon her hands are moving up and down, up and down, and then a little higher to graze my cock head—that's when I pump my hips, needing to be in her mouth, needing to fuck her mouth.

I open my eyes and look down.

Her body has gone still.

And then, with small, quick flicks of her tongue, she slides it up my cock from my base to just below my head. Up a little higher to let the wet, hot abyss of her mouth hover over my tip.

I look down another time.

Again she has gone still.

I lick my lips.

Blink.

Wait.

Wait some more.

Still, she does nothing.

I can't take it.

And so I beg. "Please, Tess, please."

At last she engulfs me, takes me down the back of her throat. Tastes me. Sucks me. Devours me.

That's it.

Oh, fuck.

That's it.

Greedy, she sucks me hard, concentrating on my head, while her hand, slick with her saliva, strokes up my shaft.

Shards of pleasure spike in every single one of my nerves.

Unable to control myself, I slide my fingers into the back of her hair and anchor her right where she is.

When I give a little tug, she gasps, and this makes her fuck me with her mouth faster, harder. She's all mouth and teeth and tongue.

Pleasure coils tight and hard, low in my belly and balls. I fuck her mouth harder, faster, and I groan, or maybe roar it's so loud.

That's when she lets her jaw go slack to take me deeper. And I fuck her mouth with an urgency I've never felt before.

"Tess," I groan.

My fingers twist and tangle in her hair.

"Shit," I say, "oh, shit, this feels so good . . . I'm going to come, Tess, I'm going to come."

I prepare myself to pull out of the blissful cavern that is her mouth, but she doesn't let me.

"Fuck. Yes."

My thighs shake as my body starts to surge toward an explosion. Muscles tensing and nerves rapid-fire releasing as I get ready to come.

And then it happens.

I groan.

Wordless.

Desperate.

And I'm coming. Coming. Coming so hard.

Her name on my lips.

Tess takes everything I give her, sucking hard until I'm spent and softening in her mouth. Even then she's not done. She places small, tender kisses in the most sensitive places. And her mouth is on my balls, licking, touching, driving me crazy and sending bolts of energy racing through me.

Never wanting this feeling to end, I watch her take everything I have, and I know something about her is different.

Good different?

Bad different?

I don't give a fuck right now.

Moved in a way so unlike me, I tug her to her feet. "Fuck, Tess," I mutter, "What are you doing to me?"

"I think it's called blowing you," she laughs.

Shaking my head in amusement, I slump back against the wall and look at her. My hair is damp with sweat, my body ablaze like it never has been before, and the fire in my eyes matches what I see in hers. "Always a smartass."

She leans closer. "It takes one to know one."

That's when I twist her around and pin her to the wall. My hands hold her. My mouth finds hers. My tongue probes hers. "Just so we're clear," I start, "that is the one and only time I will ever beg."

With eyes half-lidded and super sexy, she looks up at me. "Don't count on it."

And fuck, she's probably right.

If she keeps looking at me like she is right now, I might be begging . . . a lot.

Seventeen

Tess

INDEPENDENCE SHOULD HAVE been my middle name.

Hell, it should have been my first name.

Instead I was saddled with the name Mary Theresa Winters. My parents were highly religious and they wanted me to be some kind of saint. The burden of trying to be perfect in a more than imperfect world was too much to bear. Against my parents' wishes, as soon as I turned eighteen, I legally changed my name to Tess Winters.

They had all but disowned me by then anyway.

The statement is a little harsh, but not far from the truth.

To think back to the event that led to our discourse, I have a hard time believing that girl was me. What happened might not have been right, but I still believe my parents' reaction was extreme.

During the summer that I would turn seventeen, I secretly started dating a boy from church group. Fiona had gone to camp somewhere out west, so I had a lot of free time. Very quickly this boy became my boyfriend. He had a twin, and the three of us started hanging out whenever I could.

One summer night, Taylor and Tyler both came over to my house. My parents were out at a church meeting, and they'd never know I had two boys in the house. I wasn't allowed to date, so I knew I was breaking the rules.

That night it was really hot, and the three us went down in the basement to watch a movie. It was cooler down there, and without worry of my parents catching us, we could watch whatever we wanted. About an hour into the rated R movie, Tyler and I started making out. After a few minutes, he pulled back and asked me if I would let his brother kiss me too. The idea excited me, so I said yes.

That was how it started.

The next week, after my parents had gone to their weekly church meeting, the three of us went down in the basement again, turned on a rated R movie, and this time after Tyler and I started kissing, he asked me what I thought about letting Taylor feel me up while he fingered me.

Tyler and I had fooled around at that point, but we had never gone all the way. I was a virgin. He was not. I thought about what he was asking. I wasn't naïve. I knew where the situation was headed. What I wasn't sure about was if I wanted to give up my virginity to two boys.

It was different.

Then again, I had always felt different.

In the end, I agreed.

When the twins came over again, Tyler asked me what I thought about blowing them both, at the same time. I knew if I said yes, the next step was sex for the three of us. It would be two guys and me. And I didn't hate the idea, but I didn't love it either. Still, the idea of doing something my parents would never approve of thrilled me, so I told them I would, next time.

I had to ask Fiona what to do, and over the phone, that was going to take days.

When we saw each other again, I sat on the couch and the twins both stood in front of me. I took Tyler in my mouth first. Fiona had suggested I move back and forth, so I did. And I was glad I followed her advice. I liked the noises they made. The way I knew they each really wanted this. It made me feel like I had control, something I never had. And I wondered if this girl, the one with these two boys, was the real me.

The twins and I kept this up for the remainder of the summer. It was the last week before school started before Tyler had the nerve to ask me if I wanted to fuck them both. I still hadn't decided, so I told him I'd think about it. Fiona would be back the next day, and she'd be able to help me decide.

That night though, we did take all our clothes off. We'd been talking about different positions, and Taylor had come up with the idea of him going down on me while I gave Tyler a blowjob. Looking back, I never really came, and the boys came super fast. Still, at the time, I felt like someone wanted me, and that I had control. I kind of felt like me.

It was different.

And I liked that feeling.

But my euphoria wasn't to last.

My parents came home early that night, and when they saw a strange car in my driveway, they both came downstairs to see who I had allowed over without asking them first.

The humiliation still lives somewhere deep within me.

The names they called me, the looks I received, the shame I felt, it was unbearable. Any promiscuous thoughts I had been having were buried. That girl could never be the real me. She was too bad.

As a result of my actions, my parents decided to move me to an all girls' religious school two hours away. I would be attending on a work program to pay my tuition as my parents couldn't afford it, and I'd be completing my senior year there.

I didn't want to go.

I was going to miss Fiona.

They made me.

Like I said, I never had any control.

That wasn't the first time I told my parents I hated them, but it was the last.

As ironic as it is, it turns out that school might have saved me from going down the wrong path. In retrospect, I had been looking to rebel against my parents' values for a very long time, and the twins came along at the right time.

My parents never did understand me, but I know now that they did love me in the only way they new how, or they wouldn't have done what they had done.

Now, as I sit in my café and watch the color going on the walls and the floors turning from dull to shiny, I can't help but wish they were here to be part of this, just as I had wished they were at Gaspard when Ansel and I opened those doors.

There may have been many times in my life that I hated my parents, but I never stopped loving them.

The floor machine turns off and I refocus on my task at hand.

"This wood is in fantastic shape," the carpenter compliments. "I just have the back room left. I should be done by Monday afternoon."

I quickly wipe a stray tear away and stand up. "That's great news. I didn't expect you to finish so quickly."

"Nick asked me if I could hustle, and I owed him a favor."

I smile at that. "Well thank you. The floors look great."

"It's no problem. I'm glad you like the work," the carpenter says, and starts to pack up.

Nick.

Nick has been a huge help. I wanted to do this alone, but after I made over a dozen calls on Tuesday morning, I quickly discovered the lead time for contractor work is more than thirty days out.

That's when I decided to drive Max over to Nick's office and take him up on his no-strings offer to assist me in coordinating the renovations. While there, I met his two field scouts, Ash and Hayden. Between the two of them and Nick, all the contractor work was arranged by the day's end. That was Tuesday, today is Friday, and the place is shaping up quickly.

Sitting back down at my makeshift desk, I move my mouse and continue with the design template the sign maker sent to me. I have decided to call the café, 'The Press Room'. A play on coffee and the fact that this place used to be an old printer's shop. I would like a typewriter-like font so I click on my choices and watch the sign come to life, virtually anyway.

As I click font after font, my mind wanders to the past five nights. Each night spent with Nick. Each night, as soon as we got Max to bed, we raced for the spare room desperate to have each other. And each night I fell asleep with him by my side and woke up the same way.

I'm not lovesick, don't worry.

In fact, I try not to put much stock in it.

I'm the flavor of the month, after all.

Knowing me, you'd think I'd be livid about that fact, but looking at things objectively, he's the guy after my long-term relationship went bad, and by all accounts that makes him my rebound guy.

Right?

And rebound relationships never work out anyway, or so they say, but I'll take what we have until we don't anymore.

That's all I can do.

I sigh and rest my head on my chin, memories of this morning rushing back. When I woke, I rolled on top of him, and stared down waiting for him to open his eyes. When he didn't, I traced one fingertip over his eyebrows, one at a time. He smiled, and I knew he was awake. Still, he didn't open his eyes, so I drew a finger over his lips, they parted just enough for me to slip the point of my index finger inside. He bit it gently, then sucked, and the sensation sent a delicious shudder through out my entire body.

It was sweet and wicked at the same time, and right at that moment, I felt myself becoming attached to him in a way I knew I shouldn't.

"See you Monday, Miss Winters," the carpenter calls, and I shut down the thought process that will only make me overthink my situation.

Collecting myself, I twist in my seat. "Bye, have a great weekend."

"I'm leaving too Ma'am," the painter says.

I give him a wave. "I'm twenty-eight, not eighty-eight, it's Tess."

"Yes, Ma'am, I mean Tess."

I laugh. "Thanks for everything. See you Monday."

Alone in my new café, I cast aside my thoughts of Nick and I in bed and ponder what to do tonight. Nick and Max are going to Jace's for their Friday night ritual. I could go out to eat, or to a movie, but I'm a little dirty and don't really feel like getting all cleaned up to go out alone. In the end I decide I'll just go back to Fiona's. It's not even five yet though, so I think I'll finish up what I'm doing first.

Resuming plugging away at the sign-making app, I'm surprised when the door swings open. "Did you forget some—" I wheel around to say, but I am struck speechless when I see Nick standing there in the dapper suit he wore to work this morning.

One hand is shoved in his pocket. His pose is both casual and arrogant, and my breath catches. As soon as he catches my eye, he strides toward me in a manner that exudes confidence, charm, and power.

God, does it turn me on.

If someone would have asked me if I thought I'd be attracted to the alpha male persona, I would have said, "Hell no."

I'd have been wrong.

"Hey," he says averting his eyes from me to wander the space I've rented from him.

"Why hello," I say in surprise. "What are you doing here?"

Nick stops right beside me, stares down at me, and then answers with, "I came to see how things are coming along."

"Pretty good, if you ask me."

He grins knowing things are *pretty good* because of him. "Got any plans for tonight that you can't cancel?" he asks.

I purse my lips. "Depends."

"On what?"

"Why you're asking."

Nick laughs softly. "Always so sassy. I'm asking because I want to do something with you."

Surprised, I ask, "Aren't you picking up Max and going directly over to Jace's?"

He shakes his head no. "Scarlett is sick, so Jace had to cancel."

"Oh, I get it. I'm the backup plan."

"No, I had this idea in mind for tomorrow night, but since plans changed, I thought I'd move it up."

"Move what up?" I ask ruefully.

"A change in routine."

"Change in routine? What do you have in mind?" I ask huskily. The tone of my voice much more seductive than I had intended.

Nick raises a brow. "To be blunt—a big king-size bed."

I tilt my head in confusion.

"I was thinking the three of us could head to my place, order pizza, and watch a movie," he says.

I raise a brow. "Where does the big king-size bed come into play in that equation?" I tease.

"That would be you under me in my bed after Max passes out five minutes into a Disney movie."

"Oh," I smile.

He lifts my chin toward him. "What do you say?"

I shiver as our gazes meet and hold, but try to keep it light. "Sounds like fun. I'll run back to Fiona's and grab a bag for Max and I, and meet you there."

"I'll arrange for an Uber to pick you up."

"That's not necessary, I can drive."

"Tess."

I glare at him. "What?"

"It will be there in an hour," he insists, and I know arguing will get me nowhere."

"Fine."

"And grab enough stuff for two nights."

"You're awful presumptuous. After all, tomorrow night is my night off."

Nick traces his fingers around my lips. "I'm fairly certain after tonight, you'll want to stay for another night."

I close my laptop. "We'll see."

We'll see might be the words I tell him, but I want to scream . . . yes.

Hell . . . yes.

Eighteen

Tess

THE LAST TIME I put a lot of thought into what undergarments to wear, I was twenty-two years old.

Six years later, lacey bras and frilly panties aside, I no longer own any sexy lingerie, but I know who does.

After a quick shower, and way too long contemplating what to wear, I rummage through Fiona's drawers and find a number of pieces from her bridal shower with the tags still on them.

I know she won't mind.

We've shared everything but men since we were five.

In fact, she'd be tossing pieces at me right now if she were here. Well, maybe not if she knew I would be wearing the sexy number for Nick. I have no idea what she'll say about me hooking up with Ethan's jerky friend, as I always referred to him.

Nick and I have been careful not to flirt in front of Max, and to avoid talking to Ethan and Fiona at the same time in case they sense something. We're not sure how they'll feel about us hooking up while watching their son.

Hey, what they don't know won't hurt them.

And Max is being very well taken care of.

The driver beeps and I quickly decide on the black one, toss it in my bag, and start to rush outside, quickly turning back to get the red one, just in case I change my mind.

It's dark and cold, but that doesn't keep the cars off the road. Traffic is a bitch and it takes more than thirty minutes to get to Nick's apartment building, if you could call it that.

The skyscraper looks more like luxury condominiums. Not only does the glass glimmer and reflect tiny stars down onto the Chicago River, but the sheer amount of lights surrounding the complex could brighten an entire block.

I'm surprised.

Not that I thought he'd live in a dump, I just didn't think he'd live in such a nice place. In New York, I lived with Ansel in a loft in SoHo. It was nice. Hip. Artsy. Trendy. Completely Ansel's style. This place is a completely different vibe. Completely Nick's style.

Grabbing my bag, I head inside. The lobby is magnificent with its white marble floors and cherry hardwood walls. I glance down at my phone before stopping at the security desk to see what floor Nick texted to me.

"You must be Miss Winters," the older man says.

I look up. "Yes."

"Mr. Carrington told me you'd be arriving and he asked me to send you right up."

"Oh, thank you."

"Please follow me."

"Okay," I smile.

He leads me to the furthest elevator bank, ushers me in, steps in himself, presses a button, and then steps back out.

"Oh, which way do I go when I exit the car?"

He looks confused.

"Never mind. I'll figure it out. Have a good night."

"You too," he calls just as the doors close.

The elevator rises and I suddenly feel nervous. This isn't a date or anything, so I have no idea why.

As soon as the elevator doors open, I suddenly know why.

And his name is Nick.

As always when I first look at him, I get a little flutter in the pit of my stomach, and my skin tingles. This time though the sight of him causes my breath to hiccup and stick in my throat.

With his thick, dark hair and great body, he's standing at the edge of the stairs that lead to his living room with a glass of wine in each hand. He's showered, I can tell by the wet ends of his hair. He's wearing track pants and a t-shirt. And he looks really sexy.

Just behind him is Max, who is on the couch in his pajamas with wet hair too. He's eating pizza and watching television.

"Hi," I wave, setting the overnight bag down.

"Hi," he says back, stopping mid-step.

"Sorry it took me so long," I blurt out, my nerves still aflutter.

Nick's gaze burns over me from head to toe. "You look fantastic, so don't apologize. And besides, the pizza arrived less than five minutes ago."

Good, I'm glad I picked out what I did to wear. I'd hoped it wasn't too much, but by the twinkle in Nick's eyes, I'd say it is just right. "Thank you," I tell him, and I can't stop the shiver that runs down my spine as our gazes hold.

Nick seems to break out of his daze and continues striding toward me. First he hands me a glass of wine. "For you."

I accept it. "Thank you."

And then he leans over and kisses me. Max's back is too us, but still I'm surprised by the gesture, and a heated rush takes my breath away.

The kiss, although intense, is short, and soon he pulls away.

"How about a quick tour before dinner?"

I take a sip of my wine, wondering if my beating heart will continue to thump at this elevated pace all night. "Sounds great. Let me just say hi to Max."

Nick nods and picks up the bag I brought.

On shaky legs, I walk toward the little tyke, who completely ignores me because he is too caught up in television show.

While in the living room, I take a minute to look around. Everything is warm and inviting in dark woods offset by light colored walls and furniture. The walls are covered in architectural-like prints. They look to be buildings, both old and new, throughout Chicago. His place looks more like a home than a bachelor pad. Drawn to the view, I walk over to the wall of windows. "I love your view."

Nick is behind me now, and his warm breath caresses the skin of my bare shoulder. "It's not bad."

"You're always so modest," I mock.

He steps a little closer and the back of my legs graze the front of his. "I'm just being honest."

I shake my head.

Nick points a finger out the window, using the opportunity to step even closer. "See that building over there," he says.

With the pitter-patter spasms of my heart something I know I need to get used to, I dart my eyes to where he is directing. "The old abandoned plant?"

"That's the one. I want to buy it from the city and build my first residential living complex."

The excitement in his voice has me looking over my shoulder. "Would you tear it down or renovate it?"

"If at all possible, I'd like to renovate it, but it's in bad shape, so it depends on the building's integrity."

"I've seen you at work. I bet you can do just about anything you put your mind to."

There's a gleam of appreciation in his eyes, and where I thought this would be the point he'd turn cocky, he appears humble. "Thank you, I appreciate the vote of confidence."

I give him a warm smile.

Nick grabs my hand. "Come on, I owe you a tour."

The contact causes arousal to hum low in my belly.

Oh, boy.

But Nick is surprisingly a gentleman as he shows me around his place. There are two bedrooms, two bathrooms, an office, and the living room/kitchen combo. It is luxurious and warm and inviting, and I kind of fall in love with the place.

Back in the living room, Max is now vertical on the sofa, but still entrenched in his television program. After checking on him, Nick leads me toward the kitchen island.

"How long have you lived here?" I ask.

He pulls out a barstool for me to sit. "Four years. I got the place for a steal."

I look at him. "It's really nice."

Before taking a seat himself, he covers his heart with his hand. "Is that two compliments in one night?"

I bite my lip. "Yes, and enjoy it. I don't give many, so your quota is almost up."

"I figured," he grins. "Pepperoni or cheese?" he asks pointing to the pizza box.

"Cheese, please."

He puts a slice on my plate. "Ahhh . . . please. That is a word I intend for you to repeat many times tonight."

Once I chew my first bite, I lean in a little closer. "Like you, I don't beg."

He gives me a wicked smile. "We'll see."

I roll my eyes and take a sip of wine. This is going to be a fun night, I can already tell.

By the time we finish eating, we've each drank two glasses of wine and talked in depth about the various buildings along the river, which I've been to, which he's been inside of, and how the city has changed since I moved away.

After wiping my mouth, I set my napkin down beside my plate and look over toward Max. To my surprise, he is out cold. "I can't believe he fell asleep," I say to Nick, "just five minutes ago he asked for another slice and more milk."

Nick stands and clears our plates. "I guess school tired him out today. While I move him into Lucas's room, feel free to take a closer look at my bedroom."

Picking up my wine glass, I look over at Nick. "Just like that? You aren't going to use any of your arsenal of romance tricks on me first?"

His gaze narrows and he takes a step closer. "Arsenal of romance tricks? What the hell are those?"

I sigh. "You know, your game. Your technique. Bring a woman up here, show her the view, give her a night cap, light a fire outside, talk about shallow things, and seduce her into your bed, or—"

He brushes his thumb over my lips to silence me. "First of all, I don't have an arsenal of romance tricks, and even if I did, I would never use them here. I'm not in the habit of bringing women back to my place."

My head spins with this information. This really isn't his bachelor pad then. At least not in the traditional sense of the word. Still, I don't falter. "Why not?"

"I don't like things to get too messy."

"You mean, you like to be able to cut and run when you're ready."

"Yeah, I guess so."

I set my glass down and stand up. "And yet I'm here."

He looks down at me. "You're different."

"Why?" I ask breathily.

"I don't know."

"What if I don't want to be different?"

Nick runs his fingers over my bare shoulder. I opted for braless tonight, to make my sweater look sexier. His fingertips coast lightly down the slope, and then he draws them down the center of my off-the-shoulder sweater, stopping just below my belly button. The move thrills me. "We don't always get what we want, baby. Like right now what I want is you naked in my bed, but you want to go round for round."

This time I step toward him and bring my mouth close to his. "I don't want to go round for round. In fact, I'm really glad you invited me over," I concede.

He takes my mouth with his and suddenly his hands are tangled in my hair, yanking me closer so there is no space between us. After a long while, he breaks away and sucks in air to catch up from his kiss. "I'll accept that as an *I'm sorry* and forgo any punishment . . . this time."

Gasping for my own breath, my jaw drops open. "That wasn't, I didn't, I'm not into."

He raises a brow. "You're not into . . . what, Tess?"

"That kind of stuff," I say meekly, hating the taste of the fib on my tongue.

"You don't have to be embarrassed, Tess. I know you like it. I know how much it turns you on when I talk dirty or when I tell you to get on your knees."

Words won't form, so I say the one word that will come out. "Jerk."

He smiles in amusement. "You can deny it all you want. The truth doesn't lie."

I cross my arms over my chest.

"Oh, come on, don't be mad. Someday you'll be able to admit it, but for now, we'll pretend you're appalled by my vulgar behavior."

My eyes drift over him in mild irritation, but in the end, I can't stop from allowing my lips to turn up, just a little.

At that he swats my ass. "I'll grab us a brandy as soon as I tuck Max in, and we can . . . talk."

Not entirely certain I want to have the conversation about kinky sex, I think about what it is we should talk about. In the end, I decide to let it be, and ask, "Do you want some help?"

Nick gives me a sly grin. "No, I got it. You just make yourself at home."

I watch him pick Max up, all six-foot-two, or maybe three inches of him, and think *he's right.*

I do like it dirty.

I do like it when he commands me.

I do like it when he takes control.

Actually, it thrills me.

The twins come to mind, and the precariousness I was feeling when I was seventeen that I thought I had buried. Maybe it was under the surface, but perhaps it could never really be suppressed.

The truth very well could be that I'm just a dirty, dirty, girl.

And I've never been willing to admit it . . .

Until now.

Nineteen

Tess

WITH EACH STEP I take, his words echo in my head, *'You're different.'*

I want to know why.

How?

But at the same time, I don't want to know. The thought of what the answer might be terrifies me. He terrifies me. Am I like him? Is he like me? Is he different too?

With way too many unanswered questions in my head, I find myself in the doorway to his bedroom, staring at his luxurious bed with its masculine wooden bed frame and majestic four posts.

I want what he wants.

So why am I fighting it?

My bag is beside me, and I grab it. Once I walk to the bathroom, I set it down, and open it. That's when I pull out both pieces of lingerie.

Red or black?

I can't decide.

I hold the red one up and look in the mirror, and then I set it down and hold the black one up.

"Did you change your mind about the drink?" His husky voice fills the large space.

Startled, I jump a little and slowly turn toward him. "No. I just thought I'd slip into something more comfortable before we . . . talk."

Leaning against the doorframe, he stares at the item in my hand. "Having a hard time deciding?"

I stare at him through the reflection in the mirror, and for some reason, another flutter of nerves awakes in my belly. "As a matter of fact, yes, I am."

"Would you like my opinion?"

I shake my head. "No, I think I can decide which one to wear."

He crosses the distance between us rather quickly. And then he's behind me. The heat of him presses against my back, and his hot breath whispers across the back of my neck. "I like the black one."

Wadding the fabric up into a small ball, I fist it in my hand, and look at him in the mirror once again. "I'll take that into account."

Nick slowly slides his hands under my sweater. "Good," he breathes and then even slower he pulls my sweater over my head. "I like when you have an open mind."

As soon as the cool air hits me, my breasts swell and my nipples peak.

Nick isn't done yet though. His hands slide down to my hips, and he grips them, gently pulling me back against him so I can feel the hard, rigid length of his arousal against my bottom.

Our eyes are locked in the mirror and I watch him as he sweeps my hair off one side of my neck to allow his hot lips to brush over my ear. "You're driving me crazy," he confesses.

His words elicit a moan of pleasure from me, and I grind myself against his erection. "Maybe I like driving you crazy."

Still looking at me, he trails light kisses down my neck. "I'm sure you do."

His touch sends a thrill coursing through my body.

Slowly, he slides his hands down to the zipper of my jeans, and even more slowly he unzips them, and pulls them down.

I step out of them, goose bumps rising all over me as I stand in nothing but a pair of frilly old panties.

His hands move to my hips, and cool air whispers between us as he steps back a little. I follow his sizzling gaze and watch the fire burn in his eyes, as he slides those deep blues down my body and then back up. "You're so sexy."

Anticipation and arousal are all I can feel, and I don't say a word in a response.

He steps closer again, and his heat now blazes against my back. With his hard-on prodding against me, he cups my naked breasts.

I sigh, and rest my head against his shoulder. Ripples of desire unfurl low in my belly as he plays with my breasts, kneading them, stroking them, and pinching them into hard points. I thrust into his touch, his name falling from my lips in a breathless whisper while he pumps his hips in rhythm with my own movements.

"Your mouth," he growls.

I turn my head at his demand and my lips instantly meet his. Wrapping an arm around his neck, I open my mouth, inviting his tongue inside. He kisses me with deep, slow abandon. I gasp as he pinches my nipples. His growl of satisfaction rumbles into my mouth and he coasts a hand down my stomach and over my panties. And then he rubs his fingers over them, and I think I'm the one who will surely go crazy.

When Nick discovers they are soaked with evidence of my arousal, he pulls back from our kiss. His eyes are low lidded with his own desire. "Follow me," he orders.

I swallow. "Okay," I reply, and that's when I realize I'm still holding the lingerie pieces in my hand. I drop them to the ground. I think I'll save that for another day when my indecisiveness can be cleared up much easier.

Step by step we go, him back, me forward. We move like this—a predator and his prey. He is close. So close. He takes one last step to the foot of the bed and his expression shifts from amusement to something more lustful, darker. When he stops, he tugs me to him. We are chest-to-chest, hip-to-hip and when he presses into me, his cock nudges the naked flesh of my lower belly.

I gasp, trying to catch my breath.

His lips part when he stares down.

I stare up, my own lips parting in their own breathless anticipation.

And then he kisses me again. His warm, sensual mouth working exquisitely over mine. This kiss is fierce. Demanding. Coaxing. Light flecks of his tongue wisp against mine but become harder with each passing moment. Sparks ignite and I swear my leg kicks up. I urge him for more, pushing my body so far into his we might become one.

Breathing hard, he lets me go and steps back.

I watch him with curiosity.

Across the room, he pushes a button and the fireplace flares to life. "Would you prefer wine or brandy?" he asks, still so very far away.

I stare at him in utter disbelief. "How do you do that?"

He dims the lights, but only slightly. "Do what?"

"Go from hot to cold?"

He turns on some soft music. "I take my cue from you, Tess."

"I don't do that."

He throws me a look. "Maybe not with your words, but with your body language you do it all the time."

I draw in a breath of defeat. "If I do, I don't mean to."

After a long-suffering sigh surely meant for show, he says, "It's something for us both to work on. Now, do you prefer wine or brandy?"

Hoping his little lesson is over, and he's ready to resume what he started, I answer his question. "Nothing, thank you." My voice is nothing more than a rasp. "I think I'm good."

And still, he keeps his distance. "Anything else I can get you?"

I consider covering myself, but that would only give him satisfaction. "No."

"Are you sure?"

"Yes, what is going on, Nick?" I ask.

"I just want to make certain I get this right. Is this enough romance? Enough game?"

I get it now, and I ignore the teasing taunt in his voice. "Yes," I sigh, and then add, "And I'm sorry about that."

His gaze darkens. "You're sorry?"

"Yes, I am. Now please come back here."

Nick tosses me a wicked grin, and finally he moves closer, but still he doesn't touch me.

"Please."

At that, he takes my head in his palms and his lips make their way down my throat. "See how easy things can be when you're nice?"

I make a noise of irritation mixed with passion.

Nick gives a huff of laughter, and I laugh along with him.

Seemingly moving past our control issues, he silences me with a deep, drugging kiss. When he slides his tongue to my ear, he whispers, "I've been waiting for this all day."

I throw my head back when his mouth moves lower. "Me too."

He kisses my bare shoulder. "Were you really thinking about this?"

I close my eyes. "Yes."

He kisses my breast. "Tell me what you imagined I'd do to you tonight?"

I shiver in delicious delight. "What you're doing right now."

Nick takes a step forward, and I'm forced to step back. "Were you naked when you thought of the two of us?"

I nod, and stare up at him. "And so were you."

His gaze goes black with heat. "Take your panties off. I want to see all of you," he growls.

I do.

The hissing sound he makes is reward enough for complying without the cheeky banter we both seem so intoxicated by, but the way his fingers press against my now exposed clit, drives me out of my mind.

"Oh God." I slip my hand over his, wanting more than he's giving me.

This apartment is laid out much different than Ethan and Fiona's house, and I know with Nick's door closed, I can be loud and I won't wake Max.

Nick shakes his head and brings our hands to my face, where his thumbs brush over my cheeks. "Patience, beautiful. I plan to take my time with you tonight."

I want to argue. To tell him I need him right now, but just as I open my mouth, he leans down and takes my mouth. I wind my arms around his neck and my fingers in his hair.

Moments later, Nick breaks the kiss, but only to lift me and drop me on my back across the middle of the mattress. "You're so fucking beautiful. Spread your legs, I want to look at you."

With my arms above my head and my hair flamed out beside me, I stare up at him, panting, my whole body on fire as I open my thighs.

His eyes devour me, raking over me as I lay naked across his bed. "Your pussy is perfect. Do you want me to taste some of your perfection?"

My breath hitches, and I nod.

His grin is wicked. "Use your words, Tess. Tell me, you want me to eat your perfect pussy."

"Yes, Nick, I want your mouth on me."

He grabs hold of my ankles and pulls me to the edge of the bed. "That's good, Tess, but how about you make it a little dirtier. Make me believe it."

I already told him I'm not kinky, but the words get stuck in my throat. I can't say them.

Maybe because I don't believe them?

Who cares anyway, he knows what I want.

Then I think, maybe he's making sure I know it too.

And besides, if I didn't before, I do now.

That's when the words finally come to me. "All day long I couldn't stop thinking about you fucking me with your mouth. I imagined you came to see me on your lunch break, and that you whisked me away to the bathroom, where you lifted my skirt and fucked me with your tongue until I came all over your face."

His exultant groan echoes around the room, and then let's go of my ankles. "Stand up," he orders.

The tone of his voice makes my pulse race, and I scurry as fast as I can to stand up. Just as I do, he takes a seat, like a king, sitting on his throne. I have the oddest urge to put my hands behind my back, so I do.

"That's it, Tess," he says, grabbing my hips and moving me between his legs. Once I'm in place, he drops to his knees where he places his mouth on my pussy and his hands on my ass. His fingers skate up the middle and back down. Over and over. All the while, kissing my soft flesh lightly.

"I want to make you feel good." His voice grows hoarse. "Do you want that?"

"You know I do."

He nips at my inner thigh. "Say yes, Tess."

I throw my head back. "Yes."

I can feel his grin. "That's what I want to hear. Now I'm going to lick you, suck you between my lips, taste you, eat you until you scream."

My breath catches on his words.

True to his word, he starts to suck and lick me, and the muscles in my thighs begin to tremble and tighten. Then he slides a finger inside me, and I wonder how it is something like this has never felt this good before.

"Oh, God, yes," I whimper. "I don't think I stand much longer."

I'm on my back in a hot minute, and he's hovering between my legs with his mouth on my bare flesh and his tongue circling my clit.

His tongue slides inside me, fucking me in slow, sensual strokes. Over and over, he continues to lick and suck me. Soon, I arch in ecstasy and cry out as the sensations take over me and I have to remind myself to breathe.

"Come for me," he says huskily, raising his head to look up my body.

"I want to wait and come with you," I pant, writhing in pleasure beneath him.

"Come all over my mouth, Tess. I'll work you up again, I promise."

"Okay," I moan when he slides his tongue back inside me, fiercer than before, as if tasting me from the inside. "Yes," I moan even louder when he slips his thumb over my clit, rolling it as he continues to lick and suck in perfect rhythm.

"You're so tight. So wet. So ready," he groans.

I close my eyes as I start to lose myself.

I clutch the sheets.

Just then my ass comes off the bed, and I thrust upward at the pressure he exerts with his thumb. "Now, Tess," he growls. "Let go."

He strokes me with his thumb and his fingers and his tongue, and I am unable to hold back any longer. I come in a hard rush, going wild beneath him. My inner muscles clamp around his fingers, my legs close against his head, anchoring him to me, and my toes curl as pleasure rips through me. I roll my hips and buck, as wave after wave of my orgasm takes control of me.

I know it is so cliché when a woman says she sees stars, but I see stars, the moon, and every planet in the solar system. I never want this amazing feeling to end. When I finally stop moaning and float down to earth, he pulls his face away from my pussy.

I miss his warm breath there immediately.

Standing in front of me, he leans down and places his palms on either side of my shoulders, and then he kisses me.

Pulling back slightly, he stares into my eyes. "Do you taste how sweet you are?"

Heat rushes to my cheeks.

He lifts my chin. "Don't be embarrassed. You taste like sweet honey, and I want you to taste it."

I sigh and slide my hands over his shoulders. "Take your shirt off."

He laughs, "Round two?"

I nod. "You promised me you'd make me come again, this time I want you to do it with your cock."

He raises a brow, impressed with my dirty talk. "If you insist," he says, pulling his t-shirt off and tossing it to the ground. He then drops beside me so we are facing each other and I run my fingers down his smooth chest, tracing every line and muscle. When I reach the top of his jeans, I look at him.

His face is filled with desire.

"Take your pants off."

His eyes sparkle with amusement as he lifts his torso and lowers them, kicking them off easily. Immediately, his cock stands straight up. He is long and hard and beautiful. And I can't wait to touch him. I have him in my hand and am stroking him before he has even laid back down.

He covers my hand with his. His hand moves mine, up and down his erection in smooth even strokes. I wouldn't have ever thought I could be even more turned on, but my sex clenches as my palms rub over his silky smooth shaft.

After allowing me to stroke him a few more times, he reaches over to the bedside table and pulls out a condom. "Fuck me," he says to me as he rips it open.

I can't wait.

As soon as he puts the condom on, he pulls me on top of him. I am on my knees and stare down at him. At his flat belly that is tight with muscles. At his strong arms. At his face. At him.

Just him.

He positions himself with ease and I lower myself down. He fills me and it feels so good. His hands are on my hips and he guides me. Moving me up and down—slowly at first, then faster, much faster. His hips are surging forward. He is groaning. I'm moaning as my lower belly coils with tension and my thighs begin to vibrate.

His hands shift a little and he lifts me off him, his cock is so hard it must be painful. "Lie on your stomach, I'm going to make you come even harder this time."

I don't even hesitate. I flip over quickly.

He gets off the bed and pulls me toward him. "Get up on your hands and knees, baby."

Baby.

That's twice.

I like it.

I look over my shoulder and see him grasping his cock with one hand, and then I feel him spreading me open with the other. He then positions himself at my pussy and pushes in so slowly it almost hurts.

In and out.

In and out.

Slow.

Delicious.

As he thrusts deeper, his hand goes to the crease in my ass, and he circles me with his thumb. The new sensation has my pussy fluttering. "Do you like this?" he whispers leaning over my body and into my ear.

"Yes," I cry out.

"I want to take it. Have you ever had anyone there?"

I shake my head no.

"Do you want me to fuck you there someday, Tess?"

"Yes," I cry out again.

"Soon," he growls in my ear. "Very soon."

His thrusts grow harder and faster with each passing moment. He reaches underneath me, circling my waist, his fingers splaying wide against my belly. Then he lowers his fingers, delving into the folds of my pussy. As soon as his finger brushes over my clit, I cry out, "Oh God, yes, Nick, yes."

The moment I scream out his name, he thrusts harder and deeper. He's now stroking my clit with more pressure, and then he presses his thumb against the pucker of my ass with the other. That's when I fly over the edge.

I've had hundreds, maybe thousands of orgasms in my life— never have I had one like this.

My hands ball into fists and I scream out—loudly.

"Fuck," he hisses as he stills his body.

My body shakes and trembles and I collapse on the bed. Nick follows, laying his chest on my back and kissing my shoulder.

"Oh, my God," I manage.

"You feel like heaven," Nick grunts.

"I've never come like that before. That felt so incredible," I whisper.

"I know the feeling," he admits.

Silence falls between us as we struggle to catch our breath. Neither of us delve into our orgasms any further.

Then Nick shifts, pulling out of me, and we both moan.

Soon, too soon, he stands to dispose of the condom. "Are you thirsty?" he asks.

I shake my head no.

While in the bathroom, I hear him turn the shower on, and I'm surprised when he comes back into the bedroom right away.

He extends his hand. He is so close to me I can see the blue glimmering in his eyes from the faint light illuminating the room. "Come on, let's take a shower. It's early still, so I have plenty of time to romance you properly."

I accept his proffered hand. "Nick, please stop teasing me about that. I didn't mean it that way at all."

"Does that mean you don't want to sit outside beside a fire with a glass of wine and enjoy the view?"

I step toward him. "No, that doesn't mean that."

"Does that mean you don't want to be naked under a blanket while I feast on your sweet pussy again?"

Laughing now because really, he is taking things too far, I step even closer and jump up, wrapping my arms and legs around him. "I definitely didn't mean that."

Firmly holding me, his thumb strokes up the crack of my ass and once again circles the puckered area. "Does that mean you don't want me to do this?"

I press my face against his shoulder and bite down in pleasure. I had no idea how good that could feel. "No, it doesn't."

"You like that, don't you?"

I nod. "Very, very much. Not only do you have a magical tongue, but magical fingers too."

He nips at my lip. "And penis."

I nod.

"Say it, Tess, I want to hear the words."

I giggle. "You also have a magical penis, Nick Carrington."

"Good. Now that we got that straight, there should be no more problems between us. Do you want to get started on the magic penis right now," he says, circling my puckered skin.

I shake my head no.

He circles his thumb and I press my soaking wet pussy against him. "You sure?"

I nod. "One earth-shattering experience a night is all I can handle."

"Earth-shattering? Say that again."

I bring my mouth to his. "Shut up and kiss me."

"Say please."

"Please," I breathe out.

"You're learning," he says, and then his mouth is on mine, owning me, and taking my breath away.

For sex with Nick, I will learn to say please.

With Nick, I might even beg.

Twenty

Nick

FOR AS LONG as I can remember I've always been somewhat of a selfish prick, especially in the sack.

Sure, I liked to get women off, but only because I knew it would make my orgasm that much sweeter.

Getting Tess off though, that is something I can't get enough off. The sounds she makes. The way she moves. The way her body responds. Her orgasms are like a drug, the more I get, the more I want.

And when she gets me off—fuck, it's like nothing I've ever felt.

Today is Monday, and Tess had Max for the morning while I went to work. I knew she'd be taking him to preschool around eleven, so I called her and asked her to drop back by Fiona and Ethan's place for a quick second before heading to the café. Max was being a chatterbox, so she didn't play fifty questions or try to argue. I'm sure she thought it would be easier just to do as I asked. And yes, she's learning, and yes that made me smile.

The reason for the quick rendezvous—I had a gift for her, well actually two.

As soon as she walked up the stairs she saw it. The old-fashioned cash register she wanted for her café. I had put a bid on it last week on eBay, won the auction, and it arrived this morning.

Now, she's thanking me, on her knees in front of me.

I slide my hands through her hair, curling the strands around my fingers as I lean into her. Deeper. Each movement bringing pleasure that sets me on fire.

I've been with many women, that is no secret, but Tess is different. I can't explain it, and for now, I don't want to dive too deep. All I know is that when we're together we talk about things I have never talked about. We laugh more than I ever remember laughing. And our chemistry in bed is off-the-charts.

I think I now understand the meaning of the phrase, 'pussy-whipped."

My pants are at my ankles, the belt jingling against the floor as I sink into her mouth, hitting the back of her throat before sliding back out.

She licks her tongue over the sensitive underside of my cock and I groan, "Fuck, that feels so good. I don't think I've ever felt anything better than your mouth around my cock."

I can feel her smirk.

This time as she slides her mouth over my cock, she takes me so deep that I can't hold on to my sanity any longer.

"I'm going to come, baby. What do you want to do?" I ask in a strained voice.

Her answer comes when she puts her hands on my ass and holds me to her mouth, milking my cock for everything I have.

And then I come and come and come.

Once I'm spent, she tears her mouth away from my cock and stares up at me. "Well, that was unexpected."

I cup her face in my hands, and pull her up to me. "Yeah, but

I'm not complaining. It's not like I was going to turn your offer of a blowjob down."

She bats my chest with her tiny fist. "I think being around you is turning me into a sex addict."

"Ouch," I joke and yank my pants up. Once I button them and fasten my belt, I reach around to the bag on the counter and hand it to her. "I got you one more thing."

Suspicion looms in her eyes as she takes it. Slowly she opens the bag and pulls the rectangular box of lubricant out. She shakes her head at me.

"What?" I say, "I thought we could get started on what we talked about the other night."

"How do you know I'll be in the mood for sex tonight?"

I pull her close and place my hands on her ass. "Because we only have two nights left before our babysitting gig is over and I know you'll want to make the most of it."

Tess pushes away from me and tosses the lube on the counter. "Is sex the only thing you ever think about?"

She doesn't look at me. She gives me her profile, staring into the kitchen.

When she finally meets my gaze, her eyes are blazing with some unnamed emotion. I stare at her, wondering where the hell this is coming from and answer honestly, "It's not the only thing, but it's right up there with business and basketball."

The smell of her perfume wraps around me as she brushes past me. "I have to go and check on the contractors at the café."

"Tess, wait," I call out. "What's wrong?"

Over her shoulder she says, "Sometimes you really are a jerk."

Infuriated, I take a tentative step to go after her, but decide against it. Instead, I stand at the counter, stunned that she just walked out on me.

What the hell?

Twenty-One

Nick

I STRIDE INTO the building and ride the elevator up to my floor, still feeling pissed as hell about what happened with Tess.

The office is quiet. Everyone must be at lunch or out scouting. Frustrated, I toss my coat on the rack. Striding across the room, I slam my briefcase onto my desk and then flop down into my chair.

Before I can stop myself, I pull my phone out of my pocket and consider calling her. I bring up her number, but can't bring myself to hit the call button. I switch to text and hover my fingers over the keypad. Words escape me. Nice ones anyway.

Dropping it to my desk, I look at the stack of notes, list of calls that need returning, and documents that should be signed. Leaving everything untouched, I lean back in my chair replaying the events of the past hour in my head.

What the hell did I say?

Or not say?

The knock on the door forces me to stop thinking about it. I glance up to see Hayden with a worried look on his face.

"What's up?" I ask.

He shoves his hand through his hair. "We need to talk."

"Sure, come in and sit down."

The chair is opposite my desk, and Hayden takes a seat.

"What's going on?"

He sighs. "I hate to bring this up, but Ash and I think you should know what's going on."

I steeple my hands together. "That statement infers there is something going on that I don't know about."

Clearing his throat, Hayden says, "Nick, what I mean is Ash and I wanted to handle this, but it's gotten too big."

Growing impatient, I ask, "What exactly is *this*?"

"*This* is Bigelow," Hayden rushes.

I furrow my brow. "Bigelow?"

"Chill man and let me explain, will you?"

I wave a hand. "Yeah, sorry, go on."

As if settling in for a long-winded story, Hayden crosses his leg over his knee. "Over the past week Bigelow has undercut the last four clients I asked Natasha to show properties to, and then he underbid a property Ash just about had in the bag. He's about to do the same right now. Ash is out today trying to salvage the bid on that old publishing house near Harold Washington Library Center that the county owns. But it seems Bigelow has someone at county on his payroll, and it looks like he's going to win the auction."

I lean forward. "Did Bigelow underbid Ash?"

"Yeah, but only by like five grand."

I take in a long breath, processing this information. "So Bigelow somehow found out what our bid was," I surmise.

He nods.

"You think Bigelow is messing with us or just doing business the way he does business? It's inevitable that we're going to start overlapping soon."

"Fuck yeah he's messing with us."

"What makes you say that?"

"The only thing that makes sense is he must have found out you rented Tess that property for under market value and now he's going to show us who's boss."

I level my stare. "Then we don't let him."

As if unsure, Hayden rubs his hands down his pants. "And how do we do that?"

"Underbid, undercut, and outsmart every step of the way."

"You sure you want to do that? It's going to cost you."

"Do you have any other ideas?"

His frown deepens. "No, but going to war with the likes of Bigelow could get messy. Let me talk to Ash, and get back with you tomorrow. Do me a favor though?"

I lean back in my chair. "Sure, what do you need?"

"Can you ask Tess if she used a realtor to look at Bigelow's place or if she answered one of his ads directly?"

I twist my lip. "Yeah, I'll try."

"Try?"

"Try!" I hiss.

With amusement in his eyes, Hayden sits forward. "What did you do, Nick?"

I narrow my stare at him. "What makes you think I did something?"

Both of his brows pop. "Because I know you."

"I'll give you that," I smirk, "But hell if I did, I have no fucking clue what."

"What did you say that set her off? That's always a good place to start."

I shrug. "I don't really recall."

"Did you tell her you love her?"

My eyes widen. "What? Fuck no, we're only friends."

The smirk on his face is meant to aggravate me. "Right, and the Bulls are going to go all the way this season."

Conceding, I admit, "We might be slightly more than friends. How the fuck do you know anyway?"

Hayden's mouth quirks up even higher at one corner. "Come on dude, your voice goes up an octave or two when you talk about her."

Incredulous, I respond with, "No, it doesn't."

"Yeah, it does, now tell me what happened?"

Ignoring the grade school boy comment, I tell Hayden a stripped down version of the story, leaving out the blowjob part. I didn't think Tess would appreciate that.

With a shake of his head, he says, "Listen, man, I've been with Allie for five years, and I still fuck up all the time. But I've learned something you might want to know—sometimes you just have to say you're sorry even if you have no idea why."

I lean back in my chair. "She called me a jerk—again, and I have to be the one to apologize."

"You are a jerk," he laughs.

I flip him my middle finger.

"No seriously, she's probably feeling uncertain about what's going to happen when the two of you aren't caring for Max anymore."

All I can do is stare at him.

"If I were you, I'd start by discussing what's next, and soon."

Stunned by the fact that Hayden is giving me advice on how to deal with women, I seek council on the biggest question. "What if I don't know what comes next?"

Hayden stands and looks right at me. "Then you better figure it out—fast."

Great.

Just fucking great.

Twenty-Two

Tess

THINGS AREN'T EXACTLY going smoothly—in both my business and personal worlds. In fact, both are rather a mess right now.

Turns out the floorboards in the backroom of the café are rotted and need replacing. And the pipes are so old, they too need to be replaced. In addition, two coats of paint isn't covering up the water stains on the walls from an old leak, and the painter recommends some kind of treatment be used and then he'll need to repaint again.

All of these things require capital, a lot of capital. Unfortunately, the small business loan I applied for hasn't been approved yet. Turns out since I wasn't on any of the accounts that I managed at Gaspard, my credit hasn't been established. The loan officer isn't sure how long it will take for all the paperwork to go through. If my funds run out before the loan is approved, I will have to put the renovations of the café on hold.

That will only cost me more money.

As if all that isn't enough, whatever this thing is I have going on with Nick will probably be over by Thursday. And oddly enough, that makes me sad. I'm not ready for it to end.

It's after ten o'clock by the time I pull into Fiona and Ethan's driveway. The snow had stopped falling days ago, but the temperature hasn't warmed up at all. Fiona and Ethan's vehicles are in the garage, and I park next to Nick's Range Rover on the pavement. I'm not quite ready to brave the cold between my car and the back door, but because I am exhausted, I open my car door and make a run for it.

My fingers are already getting numb as I fumble with the key. When I finally turn it, I realize the door isn't locked.

Nick.

This means Nick is still awake.

Every night he has gotten up to check all the doors, even though I have reassured him they were locked. That's how I know he'd never go to bed without locking up.

More than likely he's waiting for me.

In the downstairs entryway, I remove my boots, hat and coat, and slowly climb the steps. As soon as I hit the top one, I see him across the room sitting on the stairs that lead upstairs. The room is dimly lit, only a single light on over the kitchen sink, but I can see him clearly. His elbows are on his knees, and his hands under his chin.

"Nick?" I say softly.

He nods, his lips pressed firmly together. "We need to talk." he responds getting to his feet.

He's going to break it off with me.

I nod back, knowing this was coming, but still not ready for it. I tried to prepare myself when he hadn't called or texted me all day. And I couldn't believe how much I missed hearing his husky voice or reading his funny emails, his lewd innuendoes, and his dirty text messages. I've grown used to them over the past two weeks, especially the dirty texts. Things like:

I'm thinking tonight while I eat your pussy, you can suck my cock.

And then there are things like this sent in the middle of the day:

I'm thinking about stopping by the café before picking Max up and finger fucking you, anyone around?

At first I'd roll my eyes while reading them. But then I would wonder if he was in a meeting or on his computer when the thoughts struck him.

Was he hard?

After a while though, I'd crave the messages. I would be at the café or with Max when I received them and pause for a moment to envision his suggestion. Shivers would usually roll over me at first glance. Once I'd calmed myself, I'd answer back with something like:

Sixty-nine—I don't think so," or "Finger-fucking is way overrated.

Despite my text responses, we always did as he suggested because come on, there is really nothing better than a sixty-nine, and finger-fucking is definitely not overrated.

Now all that will be over because I . . . I . . . I don't know what. Wanted to be more than a sexual object to him? Wanted him to say something to me that wasn't based on sex? Wanted him to—what?

That's the question, isn't it?

I clear my throat. "Should we sit on the couch?"

He nods.

We meet in the middle of the room and Nick places his hand on the small of my back. I swallow back my emotion. It started this way, and it will end this way. Seems rather fitting.

We both sit on the couch, not really close, but not that far apart. Nick immediately turns to me and allows his gaze to flicker over me for a few short seconds before speaking. "I'm sorry," he whispers.

Surprised, I blink and again swallow back my emotion. "No, I'm the one who's sorry," I say softly. "I had no right to act like that. We've been fuck buddies, and that's what fuck buddies do—talk about sex."

Nick places his hand on my knee. "Tess," he says in a shaky voice, "I'm not very good at the relationship thing. Sex with women is all I know."

I give him a weak smile. "I know that, and I never should have expected more."

He moves closer, his hand squeezing my knee tighter. "Yeah, you should have. We both know this," he motions between the two of us, "isn't only about sex. Don't get me wrong, the sex is amazing, but there is more."

Taken completely off guard by the direction this conversation is taking, I stare wide-eyed at him.

I was not expecting anything like this.

That's when he takes my face between his hands as if wanting to reassure me that this is real. "You have to be patient with me, Tess. Saying things like, 'I can't wait to see you,' is so much harder for me than saying, 'I can't wait to fuck you.' To me, they both are meant to convey the same message, but I realize you don't know that. Hell, I don't even think I knew that was what I wanted to say until about ten hours ago when you left me standing alone in the kitchen."

My stomach does a little flip, and I mentally warn myself to proceed with caution. Still, I feel a pull to him that I can't resist, and I cover his hand with mine. "I like when you tell me you want to fuck me," I joke before admitting, "but with Fiona and Ethan returning so soon, I think I just started to mentally prepare myself for the end."

He moves our hands down to his lap and rubs the back of mine with his thumbs. "I'm not planning on this ending after they return.

I don't know what the future holds. I can't make any promises, but I swear I want to see where this thing we have goes. I'm not going to tell you being with me is going to be easy. I'm a dick. An asshole. *A jerk*," he grins. "And that isn't going to change overnight. I'm unsteady. In unchartered water. And I'm going to fuck up. Can you handle that?"

I bite my lip. "I can handle just about anything you throw at me, Mr. Nick Carrington."

His brow rises. "Even if I want you to call me sir?"

With the heavy conversation over, I decide to get back to us. "I'd be happy to call you sir."

"You would?"

"Sure. As long as I get a turn at being the dominant once in a while."

He shakes his head. "No way. There are no turns."

"Sure there are. You aren't a real dom, and I'll never be a real submissive, so if you want to play the game, you have to take turns. Max should have taught you that by now."

He moves even closer and hovers above my lips. "Never going to happen."

"We'll see," I grin.

At that he tugs me to him. "Just kiss me."

And I do.

Soft at first.

Then hard.

Our mouths crash and teeth clash.

Starved for what we weren't sure we would ever have again, we practically devour each other.

When we are both breathless, Nick pulls back. "Now that that is settled, do you want to make up by sitting on my face?"

Before I can answer with an absolutely, he wraps his arms tightly around me and whispers in my ear, "Just kidding, baby. How about we get you to bed? And by bed I mean sleep. You look exhausted."

Funny how sometimes the things you wish for work out and backfire at the same time.

Twenty-Three

Nick

EVEN AT THIRTY, I'm still experiencing firsts. How crazy is that? I've never just slept with a woman—ever.

And up in the spare room, with Tess looking at me the way she is, I start to reconsider the whole no-sex thing.

But no, I can do this.

I need to prove to her she means more to me than just being someone to bang, or fuck, or screw.

Yeah, sex is on my mind.

Especially when I kiss her on the nose and slowly work her sweater upward.

"You don't have to undress me," she protests.

"I want to. Now stand still."

She does.

I tug the sweater the rest of the way and spend a few seconds staring at her bra. Skimpy, provocative, and I think new. "Did you buy this for me?" I ask, running my finger under the strap.

"Maybe. Maybe not."

I go to work on the fly of her jeans. "Always so sassy. That's what makes you fucking perfect for me."

"I don't know if you're the crazy one, or if I am," she giggles.

I work her jeans down her smooth thighs and try not to stare at her sexy panties. "Those new too?" I ask, bobbing my chin in the direction of her pussy. My alternative was to lick it, but I'm trying to be good.

"Yes, they are."

I step back and admire her. "You look incredible in them."

"I appreciate the compliment."

Feeling myself getting hard, I quickly pull back the sheets. "Get into bed."

Her eyes wide, she slides in.

After turning the light off, I pull my shirt off and shove my pants down, and then slide in beside her.

"Nick," she whispers.

"Yeah," I whisper back.

"When I was seventeen, I did something that changed my life."

I move her hair from her eyes and snuggle closer. "Sounds serious."

"It was very serious at the time. I'd met this boy . . ."

Tess tells me the story about her boyfriend and his twin brother, and she tells me about how her parents caught them and thought something was wrong with her, so they sent her away.

"Baby," I whisper, "you were seventeen and curious. Nothing was wrong or different about you, I promise. Sex is different for everyone. The couple that lives to the right might like to do it in the shower every morning, and the couple that lives to the left might only like to get it on once a month in the dark. But if you mixed them, who knows, the new couple might like to do it in public places, or on the kitchen table."

She laughs. "You have such a way, but I get what you mean.

And I know all that, now. Back then though, it really messed with me. And sometimes I go back to that dark place, and think, *"There is something wrong with me. I am different."*

I throw my leg over hers. "I'll take your different every day of the week, and twice on Sunday. It works great with mine."

She laughs even harder, and then turns to face me. "Are you serious about the no sex thing tonight?"

"Dead serious," I tell her, waffling now that she asked, but trying my best to go through with it.

She turns around and settles her head on her pillow.

I adjust my head to be closer to hers. "About the box I gave you earlier," I whisper in her ear, "I've never done that, and I thought it would be something we could experience for the first time together."

She flips back toward me again. "You haven't?"

I shake my head.

"Really?"

"Really," I grin.

"We'll have to change that, won't we." At that she twists back around and a few minutes later I can hear the soft sound of her breathing.

She's fallen asleep.

I lean over and whisper, "Goodnight, Tess," and then I hold her tightly.

Something inside me feels different.

Something I haven't felt for a woman since I was ten years old.

Something that feels an awful lot like love.

Twenty-Four

Tess

I AWAKE TO a hard male body wrapped solidly around me. The clock on the table beside me glows four fifty-eight.

Not time to get up yet.

I close my eyes tight and try to go back to sleep.

I can't.

My mind is thinking about what Nick said, and the dirty thing, not the words of wisdom. *"Now that that is settled, do you want to make up by sitting on my face?"*

Such a dirty, dirty boy.

And I already established that I'm a dirty, dirty, girl, so of course, I dreamt about what he said. The dream was so real that my clit aches right now. He proved his point—sex isn't the only thing on his mind.

And I believe him.

That doesn't mean I don't want to have it, though.

With my ex, sex was always on the fly, squeezed in here or there. I was young when we met, and still worried that I was too promiscuous, so I held back. Not that it mattered, most of the time we were like two ships that passed in the night. He came to bed when I got up.

With Nick, it's different. I like the routine he and I have created. The time we have carved out to be together in both the morning and the night.

It's nice.

Makes me feel wanted.

Horny, I push myself back, rubbing my ass against his groin. In response, he squeezes me harder, but doesn't say anything. I do it again, and then one more time.

The stubble of his jaw slides over my shoulder and then his hot mouth is in my ear. "Good morning."

I push myself back again and feel the hardness of his cock against me. "Good morning," I respond.

"What are you doing?" he asks, nipping at my ear.

"You're a smart man, I think you can figure that out."

He peers over my shoulder toward the clock. "It's early. Go back to sleep for another hour."

I push myself back against him again. "I can't."

He rests his head on my shoulder. "Why not?"

I twist around to look at him. "I can't stop thinking about what you said last night, and I keep dreaming about it."

His sleepy eyes blink a few times. "About seeing where things go?"

I shake my head. "No, about the way you wanted to make up with me."

A gorgeous smile spreads across his full lips.

"But if you're too tired, I can just take care of myself."

In a beat, he has me on my back, my arms pinned over my head, and he's hovering over me. "There will be no masturbating without me present to watch."

I look at him incredulously. "I don't think so."

He presses his growing erection into me. "I mean it. I want to know if I'm not satisfying you."

I stare up. "Sometimes it has nothing to do with that. Sometimes the itch just arises."

"Then if we're not together, call me."

I consider this. "If I can't masturbate on my own, then neither can you."

He lets go of my arms and both his brows lift. "Tess, a man's needs are different."

I rise slightly. "That is so not true."

"It is. I usually have one in the shower every morning if," he pauses, "you know?"

"If you haven't gotten laid the night before."

"Yeah," he says sheepishly.

"I guess you'll just have to change your morning routine then. Go for a longer run. Do a couple hundred push-ups. Whatever it takes to scratch the itch."

He stares down at me. "You really are a little vixen."

"Call me whatever you want," I say, "but what is fair is fair."

"Fine," he mutters.

"Good, now that that is settled, should I take care of myself, or would you like to help a girl out?"

He rolls onto his back and lifts his hips, kicking off his boxers.

I stare at him. At all his glory.

"Take your panties off," he growls.

I love when he does that.

Still smirking, I stand up and strip.

He scoots down on the bed so his feet hang off and then holds out his hand. "Crawl up and put your knees on either side of my head."

I should be mortified, but I am way too turned on to care about things like embarrassment or shyness.

When I am up on my knees, his hands go to my ass. "Now use your hands and spread your pussy wide for me," he commands in a low voice that rumbles with the sexiest sounds of sleepiness.

I stare down at him, a little uncertain. This is something I have never done.

"If you spread yourself for me, I can get to all of you. Don't worry, you'll love it when I lick my tongue all over every inch of your beautiful pink pussy, and then I'll love it even more when you come all over my face."

His dirty words penetrate deep within me and not only does my clit pulse, but my nipples peak in arousal.

Immediately, I part myself with my fingers and lower myself down. Almost instantly, his tongue makes contact with me. I jerk and buck slightly, but Nick quickly slides his hands from my ass to my hips and pulls me back down onto his mouth.

He eats me like he's a starving man. Licking, sucking, and sliding his tongue inside me and all around me. Before I know it, I'm almost out of my mind with excitement. My arms are grabbing onto the headboard, and I'm moaning, biting down on my lip to keep quiet.

And then he inserts his fingers in and out of my pussy until they are soaked, and soon he slides them between my ass cheeks and parts me there, like I'd parted my pussy. His wet finger teasing and rimming my opening. When he pushes inside the tiniest bit, I lose all control.

My orgasm slams into me and I explode into a giant ball of fire.

Once the last of my tremors fizzle out, I scoot back and sit on his torso, and then I look down. "Oh, my God."

Nick looks extremely smug, as he should. "Any chance you could ride my cock right now, the way you rode my mouth?"

I shake my head. "You have such a way with words," I tell him, and get to work doing just what he asked.

This time we both come together, and it feels amazing.

Afterward, I fall beside him, and he pulls me close enough that I rest my head on his chest.

Instead of dozing off during the time we have left before his alarm goes off, we catch up on what we missed in each other's lives yesterday.

Nick asks me how I found the place Mathias Bigelow wanted to rent me. I tell him a realtor that someone in my apartment building knew about from a friend.

"What is his name?"

"Derrick Williams," I tell him.

"Interesting," he says.

"Why is that interesting?" I ask.

"It just is," he answers.

I shrug and then tell him about the café, the issues, and my hopes the loan comes through fast.

"I can help," he offers.

I kiss his smooth chest. "I can't take your money. It's not that I don't appreciate the offer, it's just that I have to do this on my own."

"Okay, then I can do the labor. And Ash and Hayden will help, I'm sure. It might take a little longer because we'll have to do the work after hours, but we can do it."

I rise up onto my elbows. "You'd do that for me?"

"Yeah, I would."

"Thank you," I kiss his lips softly, "but let's cross our fingers that the loan comes through before we have to resort to that."

He chuckles and runs his fingers down my back. "If it doesn't, and I have to do the work, I'll be sore, and I might require nightly rub-downs. Everywhere. All over my body."

I grin at him. "I'll even call you sir while I'm oiling you up."

"Only if you ask me if I want a happy ending," he jokes.

This time I laugh, and when I lay my head back down, I can't help but wonder . . .

A happy ending.

Is that even possible for me?

Twenty-Five

Nick

THE GYM AT the Preston School looks like something you'd find on one of those reality TV shows.

Sure, there are the typical items—a trampoline, balance beam, and padded walls, but there is also a rock climbing wall and an obstacle course.

Drop off is in the gym today. Max squeezes my hand as I lead him inside for the last time. Fiona and Ethan's flight is due to land at any moment, and they'll be picking him up. Tess offered to pick them up, but Ethan has arranged for a car.

"I'm going to miss you," Max says, looking up at me.

I squat down. "I'll miss you too, but I'll be over to visit."

He frowns. "It won't be the same."

I rub my hand over the top of his curly hair. "What makes you say that?"

"Tess won't be there with you."

I crook my finger. "What if she will?"

He stares at me, confused.

He's not quite three, so I have no idea how to explain our situation. "How about I make sure to bring her along when I come? Would you like that?"

Max shakes his head vigorously.

I can't help but laugh, and then I scoop him up for a hug.

Just as I set him down, his classmates begin playing on the mini balance beam. "I gotta go," he yells taking off.

"Don't run," his teacher calls.

"Bye, Max," I say, sadness setting in.

As I walk away, I realize how much I've gotten used to the little champ. It might have only been two weeks, but after babysitting him I feel like something in my life is missing.

It **was** only four months ago that I turned thirty and thought my life would remain the same exact way for the next ten years because I like things the way they were. I believed that being single was where it was at. I hadn't foreseen ever wanting to change anything about my life.

Now, though, I'm actually feeling slightly jealous of Ethan —with his house and family.

Could I have that?

My cell rings, and as I look down at my screen, I shake off the weird thoughts. "Hello."

"Nick, it's me," Hayden says.

Still somewhat dazed, I open my car door. "Hey, Hayden, I'm just on my way in. What's up?"

"Remember those four clients Natasha showed some of our rental properties to last week?"

Hopping in, I quickly start the Rover. "The ones that Bigelow undercut?"

"Yeah, those ones. You're never going to guess who the realtor was that sent them our way?"

I pull out and head south. "Derrick Williams."

"You got it. And he's also the agent on record for the sale of the building I lost last week."

"Are you kidding me?

"No."

The roads are clean today, and I hit the gas. "How'd he find out about that one?"

"I'm not certain, but he was in the office last week. Natasha doesn't recall discussing anything like that with him, but the file could have been on her desk. All he had to do was glance down and see the address."

I change lanes and move faster. "He's spying for Bigelow. Are you fucking kidding me?"

"I wish I was. The only bright side is the prick has no idea we're on to him. He called Natasha today and wants to stop by to discuss two new clients."

A grin breaks across my mouth. "Are you thinking what I'm thinking?"

I can hear him flipping pages. "You're goddamn right I am."

The day is getting brighter by the minute. "Tell Natasha to hold Williams off until tomorrow. That will give us time to find something."

"I'm way ahead of you. I already have Ash looking for a piece of property right now to meet our needs."

At that I laugh. "Tell him, the shittier the better. Look in Englewood. And I'll see you in a few to finish discussing all the details."

Hayden hangs up and I ponder for a moment if we really want to go to war with Bigelow.

Then I think, *Fuck it. He deserves it.*

Let the game of bait and switch begin.

Twenty-Six

Tess

SOMETIMES LIFE GETS in the way of personal news.

Fiona came home from her honeymoon with the flu, and because of this she was in bed for five days, and then Ethan had to fly to Miami for three days earlier this week, and Nick worked late the past two nights.

That is how a week and a half has passed before Nick and I have the opportunity to tell Fiona and Ethan that we are . . . together.

Together.

It's the word we both decided to use to describe us.

Boyfriend and girlfriend sounded so immature. Going out seemed too casual. And the word item sounded way too old fashioned. And a couple, well, although we'd spent every night together at Nick's place since Ethan and Fiona returned, the phrase made things feel like they were moving too fast.

Together—that worked.

And so it is Friday night, and while Jace's new nanny, the one Nick suggested Jace get only after I prodded him, babysits Max and

Scarlett, Nick is joining Ethan and Jace for a boys' night out, and I'm taking Fiona out for a girls' night.

The plan is that we both tell our respective friends about our relationship while we are alone with them, and then all of us will meet up at a club later tonight.

Fiona and I agreed to meet at RPM Steak in the River North neighborhood at seven. This gives me just enough time to go back to my apartment, which I haven't been to in days, and shower and change.

Feeling on top of the world, I stop at the door and look over my shoulder to give the café one last look around. With the loan money having been secured just yesterday, things will start moving fast next week. I should be able to have all the equipment and fixtures delivered, the menus printed, and I can start hiring the staff.

The brutal chill hits me as soon as I pull the door open. Quickly, I turn with my key in hand and lock it. Just as I'm about to rush around the block to the lot my car is parked in, I notice a black line drawn through one of the help wanted signs posted on the large window.

I'd advertised online and in the paper of course for the chef position, but the rest of the jobs weren't as crucial, so earlier today I'd hung a couple of signs inside the café windows.

Walking up to the window, I look closer at it. The sign had read, "Help Wanted. Come inside to inquire." Now it reads, "Help Wanted. Go to 6959 S. Elizabeth Street to apply," and the other sign is gone."

Odd.

Someone obviously thinks they're being funny by sending my potential employees to Englewood.

I wrinkle my nose in annoyance.

Backing up, I go inside and tear the sign down, tossing it on my makeshift desk. Tomorrow or Monday I'll have to purchase some more. For now though, I focus on getting home.

I'm nervous about telling Fiona.

Back at my small apartment, I shower, and then contemplate what to wear. For some reason I want to look extra nice tonight, so I decide to go ahead and dig through a couple of unopened clothing boxes to find something shimmery and sexy. Having lived in New York City for so long, I had acquired a very nice wardrobe.

The nice pieces I bought, I did so at bargain basement prices. Sale shopping is in my veins. The nice pieces Ansel bought me were of course from Barneys.

Ansel liked me to look like an uptown girl. He chose to ignore the fact that I was anything but. Hey, I grew up in a dysfunctional family that lived at best in a middle class neighborhood. That fact couldn't be changed.

Talking to him though, you'd think I grew up in the hood. And perhaps he wasn't that far off.

Regardless of what clothes were on my back, I knew I wasn't the girl he wanted me to be. How could I be when he wanted me to be who I wasn't.

Looking back, he wasn't that much different from my parents, I just never saw it back then.

But I do now.

Shaking off the memories, I continue my search. Once I find a top that is perfect, I get dressed and put my makeup on. Then I play with my hair a little, leaving it loose and wavy. Next, I slide into a pair of sexy pumps that make my legs look even longer, and hope like hell I don't slip on the ice. Opting for my short leather jacket, I shrug it on and then pull up the Uber app on my phone. Within five minutes, I'm on my way to meet Fiona.

The restaurant is loud and packed. I glance around and spot, Fiona talking to the guy at the reception counter. I make my way toward her and watch as the guy laughs at whatever it is she's telling him, and then he grabs two menus. I shake my head—she has always been such a flirt.

"Hey, I'm here." I tap her on the shoulder.

"Tess," she says with a huge grin on her face as she turns around to hug me.

When she pulls back, she looks me over and then gushes, "Wow, you look incredible."

Fiona, of course, looks like a sultry movie star, like she always does. Picture Scarlett Johansson from head to toe, and you've met Fiona's doppelganger. Me, I look more like Katie Holmes. "Stop," I tell her.

"It's true."

"Thank you. And you look fantastic. I think Fiji was just what you needed."

"Can I show you to your table?" the guy Fi was flirting with asks her. Now he looks like Orlando Bloom.

"He's cute," she mouths on our way to the table. "And he's single."

Oh, my God, she's trying to set me up.

"Your server will be with you shortly," he tells us as we both remove our jackets and slide into the booth.

"Thank you," Fi smiles at him. And then she bobs her chin in my direction. "This is my friend, Tess. Tess this is Drake."

"Nice to meet you," he tells me.

"Likewise," I smile.

He stares at me a few seconds before leaving.

Fiona settles into her seat and pulls off her leather gloves with a dreamy sigh. "To be single again."

"Fi," I warn, and seriously consider leaving my own gloves on to disguise the sudden trembling of my fingers. This is going to be so much harder than I had practiced.

"What? He's the restaurant manager. He's perfect for you."

I laugh and shake my head. "You got the manager to bring us to a table."

She smiles, her glossy lips more prominent with the tan on her face. "He was standing there, so I started talking to him. Then one thing led to another."

I reach across the table to squeeze her hand. "Fiji was good for you. It's great to see you smiling. You seem like your old self again."

She squeezes my hand in return. "I feel like my old self. And I'm so glad you're back in Chicago."

"So am I."

"Are you really?"

"Yes."

She looks me over, as if doubting me.

"Fi, I'm fine. More than fine. And don't worry, I plan to stay here."

She nods. "Well that's good because you look it."

After the server takes our order, and delivers two Japanese High Balls, courtesy of the restaurant manager, I lean across the table. "So, Fiona, tell me. How was your trip?"

"It was better than I ever could have imagined." Fiona says this with gleaming eyes and lips wet from where she's licked them. "Ethan splurged for a private villa, and we had our own swimming pool just steps away from the beach. I felt like a queen."

I take a sip of my drink, and then set it down. "And, what did you two do for fourteen days?"

She puckers her lips at the tart taste of the drink, but then swallows a healthy sip. "Not bad," she says. "What did we do?" she repeats tapping her fingers on the table. "Let me see. We walked on the beach, jet skied, swam in the ocean, and lounged by the pool. We had massages in our bedroom. Ate the best food, and drank all day long. And we had sex, like five times a day."

I practically spit out the cherry I am chewing from my drink across the table. The romantic picture she'd created in my mind of the Tokoriki Island Resort somehow seemed insignificant. "Five times a day?"

She nods her head, her honey-blond hair falling just so over the shoulders of her soft, emerald green silk top. "Everywhere."

Just then the server delivers our sushi. I wait until she's cleared the area and once again lean across the table. "Tell me more."

With her chopsticks, she dips a piece of spicy tuna into the soy sauce. "The room was so romantic, Tess. It had a white sheer curtain all around it and the view out to the ocean was to die for. Everything about the resort was magical. Ethan and I couldn't keep our hands off each other. We had sex in our room, in our pool, on the beach, and in the ocean."

"I can't believe you did it morning, noon, and night," I say around a mouthful of sushi. "I wasn't sure Ethan had it in him."

She points her chopsticks, the ends stained with soy sauce, at me. "To be honest, I didn't either. He even tied me up one night and we," she lowers her voice to a whisper and looks around, "had anal sex."

This time it's a piece of rice I choke on. "Did it hurt?"

Fiona and I have always talked about sex candidly. She's the one who told me what to do with the twins the first time I put my mouth on them. She was promiscuous. Then again her parents were kind of hippies, and the camp they took her to each summer was more like a commune. Fiona told me the married couples there would exchange partners. My parents would have died if they knew. I guess her parents had somewhat of an open marriage. But even that didn't keep them together. After Fi graduated high school, they divorced and both moved away. Her mother now teaches yoga in Monterey and lives with her girlfriend. Her father remarried and has six kids and lives in a little town along the coast Washington. Fiona hasn't seen either of them in years.

Whereas I always yearned for the wild, she dreamed of the tame, but when you put the two of us together, she was always the wild one, and I was the tame one.

Fiona licks her chopsticks seductively. "At first, it did, but it didn't take long for the stretching and burning sensations to fade, and then I didn't mind it."

I stop with a piece of sushi halfway to my mouth. "Mind it?'

She shrugs. "I think it's one of the things men like to do to feel like they own you. I didn't love it, but Ethan did. I'll do it again if he asks."

I laugh so loud I'm surprised the other diners don't turn their heads. "Fi, you are too much."

"Hey, we both want to keep each other happy."

I raise a brow. "Is Ethan on that page?"

"He is now," she grins. "We talked a lot on this trip about making sure he makes time for me. I think he finally gets it. And will do it."

Our dinners arrive and we spend most of the meal talking more about Fiji, and Fiona and Ethan's sexual exploits.

They did some crazy things like watch a guy jerk himself off under their outdoor shower. I guess he'd thought their villa was his. I laughed when she told me he opened their door to see them both staring at him, and screamed before running.

Story after story, she never stopped amusing me.

I draw my fork through the last of my garlic-parmesan potatoes, but then set it down. "I'm full."

Fiona pushes her plate forward slightly. "Me too. I ate way too much."

I wipe my mouth with the napkin and consider how exactly to tell her about Nick and I—casually, or just blurt it out?

This is so much harder than I thought it would be. Besides, I'm really worried about you Nick too. What if later when we all meet up, Nick has an aversion to being seen with me? Hell, I'm driving myself crazy. *"Do it already,"* I chastise myself.

Just as I'm about to open my mouth, Fiona waves down the server. "Can we have our check, please?" she asks her.

The server nods. "I'll bring it right over."

Fiona pulls her wallet out. "Let's head over to Studio Paris early so we can dance before the guys get there. Knowing you, you'll probably leave the minute Nick opens his mouth, and then we won't have any girl time."

Right here, this is my chance.

But instead of telling her about Nick and I, I say, "That sounds like fun. I haven't danced in ages," and then I pray Ethan doesn't text her the news before I get the courage to tell her.

Looks like I've found God again.

Twenty-Seven

Tess

THERE'S NOWHERE LIKE home.

You can take the girl from one big city and put her in another, but it isn't the same. Chicago is my home, and even though I've been gone for six years, it feels like I never left.

Arm in arm, Fiona and I traipse around the block. It's a three-minute walk at most, but both of our feet are frozen before we see the black awning with the white letters spelling out the club's name.

Studio Paris has been around for a long time, and Fiona and I came here often during college. It's one of chicest nightclubs in River North. With bottle service and an outdoor lounge, it has always drawn a crowd.

Tonight DJ Jazzy Jeff is spinning, and the line is around the corner. He's known for playing classics from the eighties, nineties, and two thousands, with a bit of techno mixed in. When I lived in New York, he'd come play at Cielo, and he'd always draw the biggest crowd. Luckily, we don't have to wait in line. Nick knows the owner, and he left our names at the door.

Shivering, we push our way inside and check our coats. The pink hue of light casting on the white leather is new. It used to be purple. Still, the place is the same. We head for the stairs and pass a bunch of giggly girls here for a bachelorette party.

I point to them. "They remind me of us during your bachelorette party."

She yells in my ear, and points to the girl with the tiara on her head. "Except I was pregnant and sober, unlike her."

I laugh. "That's so true."

Upstairs, the dance floor is less crowded. There's a lounge to the left, and the long, white leather sofas are mostly empty.

"Let's get a drink," Fiona says, heading toward the bar.

I follow her, looking around at how much things up here have changed compared to downstairs. It's nicer than it used to be.

At the bar, Fiona orders two shots of tequila and two dirty martinis. "The dirtier, the better," she calls to the bartender.

He turns around and gives her a wink. She always turned heads everywhere she goes, and married or not, she still does.

I shake my head. "Always the wild one."

"Not anymore. I don't get out that much, I might as well live it up. Ethan's the designated caregiver, so I might as well get drunk."

"Is that like a designated driver?"

The bartender sets the two shots down. "Yes, except he's on Max duty tonight and in the morning."

I lick my wrist and salt it. "How'd you swing that?"

She licks her wrist and salts it. "I promised him sex tonight and in the morning anyway he wanted it."

I clink her glass. "I like your way of thinking. Here's to having fun."

She clinks back and shoots the shot, sets it down, and orders another.

Three shots and a drink later, we are both feeling more than a little tipsy.

"Don't look now," she whispers, "but the guy at the end of the bar is staring at you. And he's really cute."

"Fi, I have some—" I start to say.

Just then the DJ starts to spin "Umbrella" by Rihanna. It was our theme song as teens, and we both look at each other in remembrance. I'd say I was going to her house to sleep over, but the truth was her parents had left her home that summer while they went to the commune, so we went out and hit the clubs.

"Let's dance," Fiona says grabbing my hand. "You can flirt with that guy later. Sometimes it's good to play hard to get. Besides, once he sees the way you move on the dance floor, he won't be able to keep his eyes off you."

To say anything would just be a waste of breath.

We make our way out to the dance floor and start to move. Bouncing and wiggling, hips shaking, it feels just like old times. We know how to dirty dance. We've done a lot of it. It isn't long before people start watching us. I think that used to be the best part of going out to clubs with Fiona. Wondering what the men who stared at the two of us dancing and having fun were thinking. Except now, as men surround us and explode into a frenzy of catcalls, I didn't think it was fun anymore. By the look on Fiona's face, neither does she.

As soon as the song ends, she says, "Come on." She takes my hand. "Let's go sit down."

Over on the leather sofa, she sits on the end and I sit beside her. She attempts to wave the waitress down, but she's unsuccessful. Sighing, she pulls her phone out of her small purse.

I can see the text messages from Ethan lighting up her screen, and I cover them with my hand. "Fiona, I have something to tell you."

She glances up. "What?"

"Nick and I are together," I blurt out.

She fixes me with her stare, and then bursts out in laugher. "You and Nick? Are you joking? You despise him. You call him Ethan's jerky friend."

I move my hand away from her screen. "I did think he was a jerk, but that was before I got to know him."

She sets her phone down on the table in front of us without looking at it. "And what? Now you think he's a sexy jerk?"

"Well yes," I tell her, "No, I mean I don't he's a jerk anymore. Now I like him."

Her hands go up rather animatedly. "Whoa, back up. Did you two hook up while you were babysitting Max?"

Uneasiness moves through me. "Yes, we did, but only after Max was in bed. I swear."

She stares at me dumbfounded. "Please tell me you didn't do anything in my bed."

I cross my fingers across my heart. "I swear we didn't. We stayed in the spare room."

She's a little bit of a germ-a-phobe.

"Oh thank fuck," she says, dragging her hand dramatically across her forehead and leaning back against the couch. The look in her eyes tells me she's processing everything. The alcohol making her a little slow to the draw.

I wait for it.

First comes the hand gesture. "Let's be clear," she says, narrowing her eyes at me, and pointing her finger. "Are you telling me you had sex with Nick, and you've waited until now to tell me?"

I nod impishly. "I've been trying to tell you all night."

Fiona continues to wave her finger at me. "Hold on. Let me get this straight. You and Nick are," she air quotes, "together."

I nod again.

"And by together, you mean fucking."

I nod one more time.

She goes back to pointing, her words only mildly slurred now. "And you let me go on and on about how many times I fucked my husband in Fiji instead of telling me all the sordid details about how the hell you ended up fucking Ethan's jerky friend, Nick Carrington?"

"For you," the waitress says to me, setting a dirty martini down in front of both me and Fiona, "from the guy at the bar."

I smile at her. "Thank you."

The three shadows looming over us should have been the first sign that the waitress wasn't our only company, but I was so engrossed in Fiona's animated question, I never looked past her.

A husky male's throat clears.

I look up to see Nick, Jace, and Ethan, but really all I see is Nick. He's wearing a black long sleeve t-shirt that sculpts his body and black jeans that hang low on his hips in the most delicious way.

Don't get me wrong, Jace and Ethan are also both very good looking men. Just not my type. They are dressed very much the same as Nick—t-shirts and jeans. I guess hitting a dive bar first hadn't given them cause to dress up. Jace is a tall guy, maybe as tall as Nick. Maybe taller. He has dark hair and dark eyes. With his broad shoulders, he's visibly fit. Ethan is a little shorter and slimmer, but his blond hair and strong profile make him look like an Abercrombie and Fitch model.

Before Fiona can say anything more, Ethan swoops down and kisses her. "Hey babe, I hope you told her what a stallion I was."

Jace thumps Ethan on the back. "Sorry to disappoint you bro, but I think your wife would rather hear about what a stallion your jerky friend is."

Fiona's gaze lifts in horror, and she mouths, "I'm so sorry," to Nick.

Nick circles around the table and while doing so, he waves her off. "Don't worry about it Fi, I'm used to it by now," and then his eyes flick to me and I can see amusement glittering in them. "Hi," he mouths, coming toward me.

"Hi," I wave, feeling a little flutter of nervous excitement in my chest. This is the first time we've been together out in public where we know people. I wonder if he'll kiss me. I try to recall the different women I've seen him with over the years, and don't recollect him ever holding hands or kissing any of them.

Ethan looks from Fiona to Jace and then back to Fiona. "Is that right?" he mutters.

While Fiona tries to pacify her husband, I focus on the tall, dark, and handsome specimen of a man sitting beside me.

"If you drink that drink, I might have to kill the guy at the bar," he mutters.

His jealously sends a tiny thrill down my spine, and my breath catches. "I wouldn't want his death on my conscience," I practically purr.

"It won't bother me," Jace says, picking up the martini and taking a sip.

Ethan sits down and pulls Fiona onto his lap. I have to say, I haven't seen him this affectionate with her since they got married. I think Fiji was just what they needed.

Nick shifts a little closer, studying me carefully. "You waited to tell her, why?"

I shrug. "I was worried, I guess."

"What do you mean?"

I lean back on the sofa. "To be honest, I wasn't certain how she'd take it. She's really protective over me and doesn't want to see me get hurt."

He grins at my answer. "You mean because I'm such a manwhore and all, and I couldn't possibly stay with you for long."

I make a face at him. "Funny."

"Well?"

I look at him.

"How did she take it?" He gives me a *what are you waiting for to tell me* look.

I shrug again. "I have no idea."

"Then let's find out."

"How?"

"Kiss me."

The pulse in my neck begins to throb. "Here?"

He nods.

"You're serious?"

"Completely."

My eyes drop to his mouth. He really does have a great mouth. It's kind of perfect actually. "Now?"

He leans in. "Now!"

I push him away. "I thought you didn't do PDA?"

I think I see a dimple flash. It's rather adorable. "That's the real issue, isn't it? You have no idea how I'll react to our friends knowing we're together, and that makes you even more nervous than telling Fiona ever did."

Feeling my skin warm, I shake my head resolutely. "You're wrong."

"Prove it to me then."

"What exactly am I proving if I kiss you right now?"

That dimple is back. "Me. I suppose. That I'm not going to throw you on the floor and walk away, because isn't that what you're really worried about?"

I lean in really close to his mouth. "That's being a little dramatic, don't you think?"

"Perhaps, but I think you get the point."

Pushing my silly worries away, I decide to call him on this PDA. "Fine," I mutter, and then I press my quivering lips to his. But I'm not looking for chaste here, so I lean even closer, allowing my breasts to brush his chest. Then to amp things up, I press my mouth harder against his, my tongue running gently across the seam of his closed lips.

It doesn't take long for his mouth to part, letting me in. I flick my tongue against his, and he does the same. Taking it a step further, I tighten my fingers in his hair and when I do, I swear I hear a slight growl.

This is fun.

Soon though, he takes control. He moves his lips against mine, slowing the pace by gently licking at my tongue and sucking on it to deepen the kiss.

Goose bumps rise all over my arms.

He puts an arm around me to pull me closer, and when he does, my chest presses against his. A growl rises from the back of Nick's throat and suddenly I remember we're not alone. Reluctantly, I push myself away.

Nick gives me a slow smile. "Did you lose yourself in my kiss?"

He's so arrogant.

"No," I answer trying to catch my breath, trying to remember where I am, and what I'm doing.

The song changes to a slow techno beat, and then I remember exactly why we just did that.

Slowly, I turn to see three shocked faces staring at Nick and I, wide-eyed with their mouths hanging open. And to make matters worse, they were all standing now.

"I thought you told them?" I whisper.

"I did."

"And?"

"They said cool, and talked about the things we always do."

"Baseball and business," I mutter.

Not one of them has moved an inch.

"Haven't you ever seen two people kiss before?" I shout over the music.

Ethan's eyes are still the size of half dollars. "I can honestly say I have never seen Nick kiss a girl before."

"Me either," Jace says, downing the rest of my martini.

"Holy shit," says Fiona, still staring at Nick. "You must really like her."

They are all still staring at Nick, who seems to be at a loss of words.

Okay, he looks really adorable right now.

Ethan shakes his head and a wicked grin spreads across his lips. "Dude, what are your intentions?"

Jace chimes in. "I think this is the only woman he's been out with that he actually knows her last name, so it should be safe to assume he plans on keeping her around for a while."

Poor Fiona is still trying to comprehend the situation.

Slowly, Nick rises to his feet. He points his finger at Ethan. "You're a dick," he says, and shifts his finger a little to the left until he's pointing it at Jace. "And you're a dick."

The two guys burst out laughing.

Nick shakes his head.

Just then, DJ Jazzy Jeff starts to spin, "Oops, I Did it Again," and Fiona goes wild. "Oh, my God, I love this song," she screams, and then offers one hand to Ethan and the other to Jace. "What do you say you two men dance with me?"

They each take her hand, like they've done this before. Ethan steps toward Nick though before leaving and thumps him on the shoulder. "Really dude, you know we're just busting on you. I think it's great. Just don't fuck it up."

Nick throws him the finger.

Ethan feigns a wounded a heart, and then trails behind Fiona, who is being led by Jace to the dance floor.

I sit down with a sigh and look up at Nick. "So, did I prove myself?"

Nick sits beside me. "I don't know. Did I prove myself?"

I smile over at him and grin. "You did."

His thigh presses mine. "So did you."

Feeling like we just hit a milestone, I start to jiggle a little to the beat of the Britney Spears classic.

"Show me your dance moves, beautiful," Nick whispers in my ear.

And maybe it's the alcohol or the high on life, but I stand up and do just that. I've never danced for any one before like this. Sure, I've put on a show with Fiona, but this is different.

Nick watches me with his smile growing wider and wider. And then he claps his hands and starts to move a little too.

It's heart-stoppingly sexy.

Just before the song ends, the lights start flickering pink and purple. And with the music pumping, and him staring at me the way he is, I can't help but wonder if I'm not falling in love with him.

I want to dance like this forever. With him watching me and laughing, I never want this song to end. But it does, and when it does I slide onto the sofa beside him. He's still laughing, and I struggle to find the air to laugh with him.

Before I have, he crushes his mouth over mine. With the scent of his cologne, the heat of skin, and the taste of him, hot and sharp—I know that I definitely am falling for him.

He slows the kiss, feather brushes of lip on lip, and the quick and furtive slip of his tongue inside my mouth.

Then he breaks the kiss, pulling back only an inch to gaze into my eyes. "Let's go back to your place tonight."

Nick hasn't been to my place yet. Not because I didn't want him there, but simply because it is a mess, and I have very little in terms of furniture. His place is much more comfortable. I place my palms flat on his chest. "Not tonight, tomorrow night, give me a day to get it cleaned up."

His lashes are low-lidded with lust as he studies me. "Okay, we'll go out on a date."

I hold his heated gaze. "A real date?"

"Yeah," he laughs, "I'll pick you up at seven and we'll have dinner at Alinea.

I lean in to place a chaste kiss on his mouth. "It sounds like fun."

"It will be," Nick winks.

I shake my head.

When the song changes to a slower one, Nick stands and offers me his hand. "Dance with me."

I take his hand and our fingers lace. "I'd love to."

Nick points to a small section of the floor that is a little less crowded. On the way, we pass Fiona, Ethan, and Jace, and I can't help but stare. Jace is as tight against her back as Ethan is in the front. The three of them are bumping and grinding and laughing.

Nick calls out to me, obviously having noticed my head craned over my shoulder. I turn back, just as wide-eyed as they were when they saw Nick and I kissing. "Did you see that?" I ask him when he stops.

He draws me close and places a hand on my waist. "They're just having fun."

I put my palms on his shoulders. "How much fun?"

After a step, he slides his knee between my thighs. "It doesn't mean anything, Tess. Leave it alone."

I move along, following his lead, in this seductive dance he's entangled us in. "I wouldn't say anything to Fi. I'm just . . . I don't know . . . curious."

Nick put his other hand on my side, up high, just under my breast. "They did the same thing New Year's Eve. Fiona just wants to make sure Jace has a good time. She knows he's not looking for a woman, or to have sex. All he wants right now is to feel like he's not alone."

My hand slides from his shoulder to cup the back of his neck.

The edges of his hair tickle my knuckles. The heat of his hand brands me through my top. And his words affect me. "I get that," is all I say, and then I drop the subject.

It isn't any of my business.

It has been a long time since I danced with a man and could see my own desire reflected back in his gaze. It steals my breath and I draw my tongue out to lick my lips.

Nick catches me, and slides his hand up my back to tangle in my hair, tip my head back, bare my throat to his mouth as he bends to slide his lips along my skin. "You look so fucking sexy tonight."

I can feel myself gasp but I can't hear it over the thumping of my heart.

The slow, sensual beat of the music has drawn a crowd, and the dance floor is packed.

Nick slides his other hand up to cup my breast through the silky fabric of my low-cut top.

Nobody is watching us.

No one cares.

His cock presses hard against my belly. The sensation parts my lips, and his gaze watches my mouth again. "The things you do to me," he murmurs in my ear.

"Tell me," I whisper back.

The crowd is all around us, and he splays his hand wide across my ass and presses his erection against me. "How about I show you."

And feeling him against me, I lose myself.

In his eyes.

In his touch.

In the pounding of the music.

In him.

"I'd really like that," I say.

His breath blows hot against my skin as he nuzzles my ear. "Let's get out of here."

I look up at him and nod.

Nick takes me by the elbow and steers me off the dance floor. We pass by Fiona, Ethan, and Jace who are still in the same place they were when we passed by them the first time.

Nick stops to whisper something into Ethan's ear, and Ethan gives us a wave. Fiona is too caught up in the bump and grind to notice us. And Jace seems lost to the music.

Once we get our coats, we step out into the cold and start walking fast. Nick has to grab my hips to stop me from stepping into the street.

"My hero," I tell him, as I turn and wrap my arms around him.

"I think you've had way too much to drink. No one has ever called me that."

I stare into his eyes. "I'm drunk on you."

He kisses the tip of my nose. "You're just drunk."

"Don't do that."

"Do what?"

"Play yourself down."

He shakes his head and then turns to hail a cab.

I watch him as he opens my door, waits for me to slide inside before he gets in after me, the way he presses his knee on mine, and just before the cab pulls in front of Nick's building, I say it again. "I really am drunk on you."

He leans close and kisses me, his reply too low for anyone to hear but me. "Sometimes I feel like I'm drunk on you, and I haven't even had a drop of alcohol."

The butterflies in my belly swarmed with delight.

Maybe . . . just maybe . . . I'm not the only one falling.

Twenty-Eight

Tess

THE LOBBY IS luxurious, the elevator equally so, with lots of stainless steel and dark wood, it catches your eye. The light inside the car is dim, and makes everything look softer than it really is. The door closes, and Nick backs me up against the mirrored wall. I can see myself in the ceiling and over his shoulder.

"Did you get my text?" he asks, looking down at me.

I shake my head. "I haven't looked at my phone since I left my apartment to meet Fiona. What does it say?"

"Read it," he says, and then drops his mouth to my neck.

I could argue and tell him it would be faster if just told me, but instead I play along and pull my phone from my tiny purse.

His hands are now roaming my body, never lingering in one spot for too long.

Glancing down, I open the text and read it aloud, "I have something for you."

Nick grins against my skin and then stands straight where he proceeds to pull an envelope from his coat pocket.

"What is it?

"Open it and find out."

I eye it suspiciously. Shake it. Turn it upside. "Can't be another box of lubricant."

Nick pinches my side. "Very funny."

I giggle a little, and then run my fingers under the sealed flap. I peer inside to see folded sheets of paper. Just then the door opens to Nick's place. I step out of the elevator at the same I pull the papers out.

There are two sheets, stapled. I move to the center of the foyer and stand beneath the crystal chandelier. I scan the first page. It is a bunch of numbers indicating his cholesterol level, weight, BMI, and blood type. These are test results from a physical.

Confused, I glance over to the edge of the stairs where Nick has already stepped down and turned toward me with his hands in his pockets. "You appear to be in very good health. Do you want me to be your baby momma or something?"

His eyes flip up. "You're quite the comedian tonight. Try turning the page," he directs me.

My eyes widen and a tiny gasp of surprise eeks out of me. "Oh," I say as I read the labels beside the test results on this page. "Gonorrhea, chlamydia, HIV. All negative."

"I thought it would make you feel better."

I reach back and take one shoe off. "About what?"

"Us."

I take the other shoe off and set them both down. "I'm not sure what you mean."

But I do.

For the second time tonight, I watch the arrogant, confident man, struggle to find the right words. This time though, it really is funny. "Tess, I never asked if you were on the pill or some method of birth control."

I drop my jacket to the ground and slink toward him with the papers still in hand. "You want to stop using condoms."

He shrugs. "Well . . . yeah."

I stop at the edge of the step, but don't step down, this way I can remain taller than him. "As a matter of fact," I tell him, cocking my hip, "I'm on the pill."

He grins. "Good."

"Not good," I say, holding up the papers. "These results need to be discussed."

His smile fades.

"Look at your BMI, it's much lower than mine, something needs to be done about that, and your cholesterol is way too low. Oh, and don't even get me started on your weight—" I can't go on, because I'm laughing so hard.

Nick grabs me and hauls me over his shoulder, lightly tapping my bottom as he strides across the living room. "You are seriously going to pay for that, woman."

I wiggle and giggle all the way to the table just outside his bedroom, where he flops me down on top of it to empty his wallet and keys from his pocket.

While he does that, I set the papers down and strip my top off and then make a move for his belt.

His eyes flare with heat. "What are you doing?"

I push his jacket off. "That should be pretty obvious. Getting you naked."

He shakes his head.

I furrow my brows. "No?"

"No."

Unwilling to accept no for an answer, I pull him in-between my legs to get at his mouth, where I punctuate every kiss with my plea. "Fuck me, fuck me, fuck me . . ."

Nick breaks the kiss and steps back.

"What?" I tease. "You don't want to fuck me right here?"

With one of those infuriating nods, he walks into the bedroom leaving me sitting on the table in my sexy new bra, all alone.

I hop down and race into his room about ready to let him have it, when I come to a screeching halt. The room is dimly lit, soft music is playing, and rose petals are strewn in a path from the door to the bed. Tears well in the corners of my eyes and I can't stop them from falling. "This is beautiful. Nobody has ever done anything like this for me before."

"Good," Nick says as he leans down, wiping my tears away. "What I want," Nick says slowly, "is not to fuck you, but to make love to you. All night long."

And if I thought just hours ago that I was falling in love with him, I now know for sure—I've already fallen. He is many things, but with me he is adorable and charming, and the breath leaves my lungs when I think about not being with him.

I nod. "I want that too."

In a heartbeat, he fuses his hot mouth over mine. Our tongues meet and slide sensuously over one another. Rough then soft.

Hot.

Wet.

Electric.

I brace my palms on his shoulders and then slide them up to his neck. This way I'm able to pull him lower. To get in his mouth. To taste him.

Slowly, we strip each other naked, and then we fall to the bed in a tangle of arms of legs and mouths.

Nick kisses me. My mouth, chin, jaw, throat. He moves his mouth over my breasts, taking his time with each one. Moves down to my rib cage, over my belly, and then back to my mouth, where he pulls back. "Tess," he whispers.

I look up at him. "Yes," I say a little breathless.

"You're doing something to me that scares the shit out of me. You're making me feel things I never have, think things I never thought I would in a million years, and there are times I want to run as far away from you as I can, but then not having you with me scares me even more."

It's called love, I think to myself, but don't say it out loud. Instead I palm his face and bring him closer to me. "I'm here, Nick. I'm not going anywhere. We'll take things slow. Day by day. And see what happens," I reassure him. "I'm not going anywhere."

The uncertainty in his eyes seems to clear, and he gives me a nod before he covers my body with his.

He shivers a little on his first thrust, and it both charms and thrills me at the same time.

We move like we are made for each other, taking the longest time we've taken to reach climax. When we are both there, I wrap my arms and legs around him and hold him tight.

I never want to let go.

Nick nuzzles his face against my neck and shudders against me. Falling beside me, Nick pulls me to him.

"Nick," I murmur.

He makes a sleepy mumble. "Hmmm?"

"Do you think everything in life happens for a reason?"

He kisses the top of my head. "I think everything in life happens, and we deal or we don't."

"So, is that a yes or a no?"

"I guess if you want a definitive answer, I'd have to say yes."

I close my eyes. "Good, because I think so too."

Yes, everything happens for a reason.

Especially us.

Twenty-Nine

Tess

PERHAPS IT IS the light streaming in from the curtains that hadn't been closed all the way last night, or maybe it is the blissful feeling of being with someone I feel so completely compatible with, but whatever it is that wakes me, I rub my eyes and look beside me.

When I do, I expect to see Nick lying on his stomach, facing toward me in sleep, but instead he's awake with his head resting on his hand and his eyes on me. "I have to go into the office."

I rise up on an elbow. "What time is it?"

He kisses me lightly. "It's early. Go back to sleep."

I stare at his scruff. "But why are you up? It's Saturday."

He rolls over and gets out of bed. "I know," he chuckles.

I sigh.

He looks over his shoulder at me. "Ash called and something's going on with the Miami deal. We need to make a call early this morning to try to get the issue ironed out."

"Okay," I yawn, and my eyes watch the muscles in his arms flex as he picks his pants up off the floor. And I don't stop staring until he disappears into the bathroom.

Feeling lazy, I plop back down and snuggle into the pillow. There is no doubt that I have a lot to do today, and that I really should get up. But I don't. Instead I close my eyes and dream about last night.

The shrill of my cell phone ringing wakes me up. "Hello," I answer sleepily.

"Are you still sleeping?" It's Fiona.

I glance at the time. It's nine. "Yes, and for those of us without a little able bodied alarm clock living under our roof, it's normal."

She laughs. "You are so right. I could have used a couple more hours this morning, but we're both up now, so lets meet for lunch. Ethan is taking Max to Home Depot to scout out his next home improvement project and I have just about an hour to hear all about you and Nick."

I snuggle deeper into my pillow, the scent of Nick still lingering, and breathe it in. "Okay, okay, where and when do you want to meet?"

"How about The Patio on N. Stockton Dr. at noon."

"Sounds like a plan. I'll be there," I say, and after our goodbyes I hang up.

Telling myself to get up and go home, I take one quick roll over to look at the empty space where Nick would be lying if he were still here, but the space is not empty. Just below his pillow is a single red rose and a folded piece of paper.

With a huge smile on my face, I grab at the piece of paper and scan the inside note. It reads,

> *Things definitely happen for a reason. Can't wait to see you tonight.*

With a sigh, I pick up the bright green stem and bring it to my nose.

Could my life actually be coming up roses?

Thirty

Tess

SATURDAYS ARE NEVER quite long enough.

Even at ten in the morning, I can already tell I won't have enough time to get done everything I want to. I had all kinds of plans for today, most of which included working at the café, but as I look around my messy studio apartment, I remember Nick is coming over tonight. My inspection tells me that just tidying up isn't going to improve this place much.

It seriously needs some personality.

I look at the boxes, the open space, the white sheets, the white walls, the bare floors, and ponder where to start. Perhaps a bright bedspread and new colorful sheets would be a good start. A throw rug or two as well. The walls will have to wait. Art is personal and can't be rushed. And of course, unpacking the dozens and dozens of boxes stacked everywhere won't hurt.

First things first though, I need to figure out what I'm going to wear tonight. A girl has her priorities.

After digging through some boxes, I find what I'm looking for.

It's a sexy little black dress. High neck. Sleeveless. The hem hits just at my knee. I slip it on and stare at myself in the reflection of the mirror. The restaurant Nick is taking me to is considered a fine dining establishment, much like Gaspard, and I wore this, or dresses similar to this, all the time. It really is perfect.

Except it doesn't feel perfect. As I look at it in the mirror, all I see is the uptown girl Ansel wanted me to be. All the years I spent working hard on establishing something that was never really mine seem to come crashing down on me. I want to rip this dress off, and all the ones like it, and shred them into a thousand different pieces.

Frantically I dump box after box, looking for something that makes me feel like me. Like the woman Nick makes me feel like. A girl who can be who she is with no care of where or how she grew up.

A small box tips over in my hunt and a bunch of photos fall to the ground. My eye catches one of them. It is from the Fourth of July Barbeque Fiona threw last year. The picture is of me and Ansel sitting in chairs on her front lawn. I bring the photo closer. Nick is in the background, standing on the front porch with a beer in his hand, and he's staring at the two of us, with almost a kind of yearning on his face.

Nick.

I crush the photo to my chest.

Nick.

He had noticed me. He had been watching me. And I had completely misunderstood him every time we were together.

I have a lot of making up to do for that.

Once I've put all the photos back in the box, I continue rummaging through my clothes, but my heart feels a little heavy, and I take a moment to text Nick. I type:

> *Just wanted to say good morning and I hope you have a great day.*

His return text is somewhat unexpected. Not dirty in the way they usually are, but rather sweet.

> *My day would have been better if I'd stayed in bed with you.*

Smiling now, I set my phone aside and get back to work.

When I come up with nothing that I want wear tonight, I grab for my phone once again and this time I text Fiona.

> *Can I borrow that silver silk dress you bought when you were in New York City last year?*
>
> *The halter one from the warehouse you took me to?*
>
> *Yes, that one.*
>
> *Sure thing.*

Ansel had said it looked like something from the seventies, then again he hated when I shopped in the garment district. He always said the clothes from there looked trashy. Funny, I wonder if he secretly thought I was trashy?

And the truth is—I don't really care.

Feeling like I have finally shed every bit of sadness I had over our breakup, I stand up tall and decide it's time to start the next Chapter in my life.

I'm more than ready.

Thirty-One

Tess

THE PATIO IS located just south of the main zoo grounds beside Café Brauer, a historic Prairie School-style landmark. Overlooking the pond at the Lincoln Park Zoo, the place is ideal for lazy Saturday lunches.

Except today Fiona is on a time crunch, and I have a ton to do. That means the lazy part of our lunch has turned into somewhat of a rapid game of twenty questions, of which Nick is the topic of each and every one.

I pluck a bread stick from the basket between us and give her a look. "Really? You've thought we'd make the perfect couple since the day you met him?"

She toys with her salad, poking at the croutons and spearing a cherry tomato. "Yes, it's true. I even told you that on the phone the day after, but you told me how blissfully happy you were, and to lay off. So I did."

I dip my breadstick in the last of my soup and then chew on it, thinking back, vaguely recalling the conversation.

"Besides," she adds, "you lived almost eight hundred miles away, so what good would it have done to try to set you two up."

I'd devoured my own half sandwich and cup of soup, and even two breadsticks, and now I am having thoughts of sampling the brownies, solely for research purposes, of course. "And yet every time I was around him, you let me call him all kinds of names, and bad mouth him."

Fiona lifts her chin, and smirks. "Hey, nothing you said was a lie. He is who he is. I knew who he was, and knew you really didn't. You couldn't though. He's not one to open up to people. He's complicated with a lot of layers."

I stack my dishes to the side and look toward the dessert case. "Complicated is a good way to put it."

"And I did suggest setting you up when you first arrived back in Chicago."

"No, you didn't."

"Yes, I did. You just never let me tell you his name," she laughs.

I ponder that for a moment.

She stabs her salad again. "Just be careful, Tess."

I look over at her. "He's not going to hurt me."

"I'm sure he doesn't want to, but Ethan says he has deep routed mommy issues, and he's afraid to commit because of it."

"And I have deep rooted mommy and daddy issues. Maybe that's why we connect the way we do."

The waiter comes back to ask if Fiona wants a box for her lunch that she barely touched. She shakes her head. "No, thanks. But we'll take a dessert menu."

I give her a look.

She raises a brow. "I've seen you staring at the case for the last five minutes."

And that is why we are best friends. We both know each other too well. Which is why I know it's time to change the subject from me to her. Something is going on with her today.

Over brownies and coffee, I can't help but notice how tired she looks, and the fact that she didn't eat anything doesn't go unnoticed either. "How late did you stay up?" I ask.

She nibbles on the chocolate. "I think five, maybe five-thirty."

"Wha-a-at?" I let the word drag out.

After she swallows a sip of her coffee, she leans closer to me. "Ethan and I were having a very important conversation."

"About what?"

"We were discussing the idea of inviting Jace in to our bed."

I stare at her. Nothing could have prepared me for that statement, not even after seeing the three of them together last night. "You can't do that," I whisper.

Her look tells me she can, and she is. "What makes you say that?"

"It's not right."

"Do I have to remind you of the twins that got you sent away your senior year."

"That was different."

"Why?"

"Because I was young and stupid, and I wasn't married with a kid."

She sighs. "Tess, you know me. You know I've always wanted to do things that aren't considered socially acceptable."

I press my hands on the table and my coffee sloshes onto the saucer. "Inviting a man into your marriage bed is completely different than kissing a girl on a dance floor to invoke a reaction from strangers."

"I know that!"

"Do you? Have you thought it all through? Like what will happen to you and Ethan after. What will happen between Ethan and Jace?"

She shifts her eyes from side to side to make sure no one is listening. "The three of us sat down last night and set the ground rules. Jace and I will not have vaginal intercourse. The men will not touch in anyway. They aren't interested in that."

"So it will be for you?"

She shakes her head. "No! It will be for Ethan and I. For our relationship. And Jace, too. He has no one."

I give her a doubtful look.

"Ethan and I want to do this, Tess, and Jace is the perfect guy. Not only is he lonely, but he'll eventually find someone to fill the empty void in his life, and until he does, we will."

I stare right at her. "I don't understand, how did this even come up?"

"When Ethan and I were in Fiji, we talked about a lot of things we never had. Don't forget, our relationship didn't progress slowly. We fucked, and didn't talk again until the day I told him I was pregnant."

"I know," I say softly.

Fiona leans forward, and continues. "He told me something he hadn't before."

"What's that?"

"When he and Jace were seniors in college, they had a relationship with a junior named Hannah." She rolls her eyes, "Hannah. That just sounds so goody two shoes."

I smirk at her. "What? Unlike Fiona, which sounds so ghetto whore?"

She narrows her eyes at me, and then laughs. "So, I'm a little jealous. Don't judge. Anyway, the relationship didn't last long."

"Why did it end?"

She shrugs. "As far I know Hannah ended it. Ethan didn't go into detail. The only thing he told me was that the three of them had decided to go skiing over spring break, and Jace suggested a place in Colorado, but didn't tell Hannah his family owed the house, until his grandmother unexpectedly showed up."

"Okay," I say. "And that was a problem, why?"

She shrugs again. "Jace comes from a very wealthy family, and I guess Hannah had no idea until then. When she found out, she felt duped for some reason. She called Jace a big shot, and left. Ethan tried to call her when he returned, but she wouldn't take his calls. Neither of them saw her again after that, and a short while later, Jace met Tricia."

"So what? Since they've done this thing before, you think they can do it again?"

"Yes, I do."

I stare at her, uncertain what to say.

"Be happy for me. I want this. I've wanted something like this since you first told me about the twins."

I give her a look.

"You know how jealous I was of you. How I went on about it for months after."

I do remember that.

"I had actually told Ethan about that time in my life first, before he told me about Hannah." She makes a face when she says her name.

My jaw drops open.

"Don't worry, he won't judge."

I keep my mouth shut, knowing this isn't about me.

As if a weight has been lifted from her shoulders, she takes a huge bite of her brownie. "Besides," she adds, "it's not going to be a steady thing. We said we'd try it tonight, and if any of us don't want to do it again, we won't."

"Okay," I tell her. "Start again, and this time from the beginning."

"On New Year's Eve . . ." she starts with a smile.

Watching the glow lighting up her face, I can't help but be happy for her. After all, Fiona didn't have to choose to settle down, she got pregnant and did the right thing for Max. She also learned to live within the constraints of marriage, which for her hasn't been easy. And aside from her adjustment to staying home, she seems to be doing a good job of it.

Maybe Ethan is more perfect for her than I thought. Or maybe he's more in tune to her needs than I give him credit for.

Either way, I have no doubts that he's the right man for her, and that he will handle the situation with care, for her, for him, and for their son.

Besides, who am I to judge?

Thirty-Two

Tess

A DRESS IS just a dress, until it is more.

The silver silk glimmers in the light, and feeling like a princess waiting for her Prince Charming, I twirl around to get the full effect.

This dress is perfect for my date tonight. Its halter-style neckline offsets the provocativeness of the open back, and the length on me is just above the knee, sexy but not trashy.

Fiona also lent me her black velvet trench coat, which when paired with a pair of black velvet shoes, looks like an outfit from the pages of a fashion magazine.

I add a pair of chandelier earrings, a few bangles, and a dab of perfume, and I'm ready with time to spare.

Then I look around my apartment, the one in which I ended up doing nothing to except shove all the boxes against the wall and throw all the clothes I had dumped everywhere into the closet.

Meeting Fiona for a one-hour speed lunch turned into a gabfest three-hour one, and then she'd forgotten the dress I asked to borrow back at her house on the kitchen counter. Because I wanted to wear it, I had to go back to her place to get it. Once there, I ended up playing with Max and chatting with Ethan.

It was five before I made it back to my place, and by then it was time to get ready. There were also numerous texts from Nick throughout the day, of which it took some time to answer. I like my responses to have just the right amount of sassy and sweet.

The knock on my door startles me. He's early. Good thing I'm ready. "Coming," I call, glancing at myself one more time in the mirror.

Quickly crossing the small space, I pull the door open with a bubble of excitement I can't contain. It's just it feels like I haven't seen him in days, even though it's really only been hours.

"I missed you," I say before the door fully opens.

"I missed you too."

The voice isn't the deep, husky one that belongs to Nick.

And that's because the man standing at the door isn't Nick at all.

Thirty-Three

Nick

THE LAST TIME I brought someone flowers, I'd picked them from my backyard.

My mother was sad that day for some reason and I wanted to cheer her up. Instead though, the flowers only made her sadder. She cried as she put them in an old glass milk jug and set it on the kitchen table.

The next day, all the petals from the flowers had fallen to the tabletop and she was gone.

I straighten my tie and then glance down at the bouquet. Tonight I'm going to tell Tess that I love her and ask her to move in with me. I know things are happening fast, but I also know slowing things down isn't going to change a thing.

She sparkles and shines and lights my world up.

She's the one I want.

The one I need.

Her building is old and a little run down, so it's no surprise the elevator is slow. Anxious to see her, I locate the stairwell and climb to the third floor. Once there, I discover I'm on the opposite side of the building than her apartment. I navigate myself up the hall, around the elevator, and just as I turn the corner, I see her, but she's not alone.

Her Frenchman is with her, and he's got his hands on her face in a loving way that makes me want to break each of his fingers. When he leans in, I want to run down the hall and punch him the face. After which, I want to throw him out the window. And then I want to fucking kill him.

Unable to believe what is before my eyes, I take a tentative step toward them. I need to confront the situation, talk to Tess, put the asshole in his place. But before I can make my legs move, he drops to one knee and pulls a small velvet box from his pocket. That's when my world turns upside down.

It's what happened with my mother all over again.

Fuck.

Fuck.

Fuck.

This is what I wanted to avoid in my life. The reason I didn't want to get attached to anyone. No attachments means never getting your heart busted in two.

I blink.

And then blink again.

My vision starts to blur when I see tears streaming down her cheeks. Soft words coming from her mouth. Him looking up at her.

She must be saying yes.

Telling him how much she loves him.

How much she missed him.

There's no doubt I'm being sucker punched.

I close my eyes. I can't look anymore.

The flowers in my hand drop to the ground.

Unable to watch him rip her from my life any longer, I turn

around and walk the way I came. A feeling of emptiness settles over me. I feel hollow. Alone.

The elevator door opens and I hop inside.

I can't even think straight.

How is this happening to me?

How the fuck did I let this happen to me?

As I step out into the lobby, I turn back around. I should go back up there and fight for her. Make her choose, but he's her past. Of course she'll pick him.

They always do.

This I know from experience.

I might have only been ten, but it was a lesson learned the hard way.

Dazed, I think my legs are moving. I can't stop the memories from rushing back. The feelings I felt those days, weeks, months, and years after my mother left us for her first husband.

Some kind of scream leaves my throat but there's no sound. I start to wonder if I'm even breathing.

Just then my cell phone rings. Hoping the call is from Tess, I reach for it. It's not her. It's Hayden, and I need the distraction so I hit accept. As soon as I do, I'm so disoriented I'm unable to say a word.

"Nick, you there?" he says.

"Yeah," I manage.

"You need to get to the airport right now. The Feds are at the realtor's office we used for the land deal in Miami and have an order to freeze the pending sale."

Work.

My life.

My entire life.

It's all I have left. All I ever had.

In a rush, I walk out into the cold of the night. "What the fuck? Why?"

"They're saying illegal funds were used to secure the land."

"That's bullshit."

"I know. We need to get down there and prove the money is legit. I got us the last flight out tonight."

I open the door to my Rover and hop in. "Text me the flight details. I'm on my way."

Once I hang up, I take a moment to contemplate what to do about Tess. I could blow her off altogether, but I can't seem to do that. I want her to see my name. Remember me. Feel something when she reads my name, even if she is with him now. And so I send her a quick text.

> *Not going to make it tonight. Something came up. I have to fly to Miami. Don't know when I'll be back.*

Feeling like my heart has just been ripped from my chest, I start my car. And then as I put the car in drive, I look up at her building. I hadn't thought much about her six year relationship with Ansel Gaspard since the two of us got together. It didn't appear that he was ever on her mind. And hence, I never thought of myself as the rebound guy.

I guess I should have.

My bad.

Thirty-Four

Tess

TODAY IS THE first day the temperature has reached above fifty degrees in five months, maybe six.

Outside, I sit on a bench beside Fiona and watch Max climb the stairs to the top of the slide.

This playground is one of the ones Nick and I took him to make a snowman. That seems so long ago now.

Fiona places a gloved hand on my shoulder. "Don't look so sad, Tess. Ethan said there's something serious going on in Miami. I'm sure Nick's just trying to take care of it, and that's why he hasn't called."

I blow out a breath and run a hand raggedly through my hair. "No, Fi, something else is wrong. It's not like him to cancel on me the way he did, and then not to text or call me either. I really think I scared him the other night when I started talking about how things were meant to be. Christ, I should have just shouted from the rooftop that we were meant to be."

Her gaze shifts from Max to me. "Stop it right now. It hasn't even been a full day since he left. Don't start thinking negatively. He'll call, just give him time."

"How can you be so positive when just yesterday you told me to be careful?"

"Because I know you really want this to work, and I want what makes you happy."

With a sigh, I pull out my phone and check it again. I've texted him and called him, but he has yet to respond.

Her voice is soft when she speaks again. "Do you think Ansel saw him last night and said something to him?"

With a shaded hand on my forehead to block the sun, I shake my head. "Even if he did, what would he say, *I proposed to my ex-girlfriend and she turned me down.*"

Fiona laughs, but then covers her mouth trying to stifle it. "I'm sorry, but how stupid was that?"

"It wasn't stupid, it was desperate. And I told you, I don't want to talk about it."

She makes a tsk sound. "Tess, you shouldn't feel bad about telling him to fuck off. He deserved it."

"I didn't tell him to fuck off. I told him I wasn't in love with him anymore. That I loved someone else. And regardless of everything, I spent six years of my life with him. If nothing else, that gives me license to feel a little bad about hurting him."

"Well, he didn't feel bad when he fucked all those women over and over, and hurt you," she mutters.

"Fi," I warn.

She raises her hands in surrender. "I'm just saying, but fine, the conversation is over. Want to hear about my night?"

"Oh, my God, I completely forgot. Did Jace come over? What happened?"

She scoots closer to me on the bench. "He got the nanny to keep Scarlett and came over around eight. We'd just gotten Max to bed so it was perfect timing. At first, the three of us sat in living room drinking a glass of Ethan's brandy—"

I cut her off. "He pulled out his brandy for the occasion?"

"Yes, he does that when he's nervous."

"So it's when he's nervous. I couldn't figure it out. Nick said he'd only had two glasses, once when he found out you were pregnant, and then after Jace's wife died."

Her face goes solemn. "Yes, after Tricia died, Ethan was a nervous wreck over how Jace was going to be handle everything. He was really worried about him."

"Wow, I had no idea. He's doing okay though, from what Nick and you have told me, anyway."

Max goes running past us over to the small jungle gym. "Slow down, Max," Fiona calls, and then says, "I guess as okay as a person can do when they lose a spouse. Well anyway, one minute we each had a brandy and were talking, and the next I just stood up between them, crooked a finger, and said come on. I sauntered right up to my bedroom without even looking back, and the entire time I undressed, dropping my clothing as I went."

I stare wide-eyed at her. "And, what happened next? Did they follow?"

She makes a little face. "At first I wasn't certain. I waited at the foot of the bed, and waited, and then I heard the soft whisper of bare feet along the wooden floor. They showed up in the doorway both bare-chested, and both fully erect."

"Were you nervous?" I whisper, although besides Max, we're the only ones out on the playground.

She shakes her head. "No, not at all. Something clicked for me right then. The sight of the two of them together made my heart pound. I held out my hands, one to each of them, and they took them. I tugged and they came toward me. I put my arms around their waists. Theirs went around my shoulders. I kissed Ethan first, uncertain how he would react to seeing me kiss another man. But when I moved to Jace's mouth, Ethan ran his hands over the slopes of my breasts and freed my bra so he could suck on my nipples."

I can feel myself getting lost in her story, and immediately get how she must have been lost to the mood.

Closer still she moves. "We spent some time during those first few minutes figuring out how to best move, and they each removed the rest of their clothes. Soon after that, four hands covered me, and I closed my eyes. Together they removed my panties and spread my legs as I stood at the end of my bed."

"And?" I bite out, anxious to hear the rest.

"Do you really want to know all the dirty details?"

"Yes, I do," I whisper yell.

She sucks in a breath. "After a lot of twisting and tangling and sucking, we settled on me kneeling on the bed with Ethan behind me, and Jace on his back beneath me."

I try to picture it, but make a face of not quite understanding. "Ethan fucked me, while Jace ate me and I jerked him off."

"Oh," I yell, and then scrunch my face and say it again. "Oh."

She nods. "Oh, is right. It was amazing, Tess. Any woman who says they'd turn it down is lying. I felt like a queen who was being worshipped by four hands, twenty fingers, and two dicks."

"Well, when you put it like that," I laugh. "And Ethan, how was he after?"

"More loving than ever. After Jace left, we took a shower and he washed me and then took me to bed and made love to me. I really think this is going to be good for us."

I hope so, I really do.

Thirty-Five

Tess

THE TEMPERATURE DROPS again by Monday.

It's in the high thirties as I make my way to the coffee shop, and my car is barely warmed up before I park in the lot around the corner from the café.

I didn't sleep. I haven't eaten. And I can't get a hold of Nick. His phone is going directly to voicemail now, so I'm pretty certain he's turned it off.

The overcast in the sky makes everything darker, especially for this early in the morning. I really wanted to stay in my bed and feel sorry for myself, but I made myself get up and go to work.

Bracing myself for the cold, I take a deep breath and open my car door. It's eerily quiet, and there aren't any cars parked here yet. I pop my trunk, needing to bring in the crate of samples I brought home and never even removed from the spot it currently occupies. I should have just left them in the café.

Before I even make it past the passenger door, a hard object runs into me. I'm taken off guard, and try to see what is happening. But my head and body are being slammed against the car. It's not an object. It's a person. A man. And he's pounding one side of my face into the metal so hard, I can feel blood trickling from my brow.

Terrified, I cry out for help, but a hand covers my mouth to stop me. Tears clog my throat and panic grips me.

A jab, or maybe a punch lands against my side and a radiating pain tears through my belly. I try to scream, but he's still covering my mouth. I try to kick, but his grip on my body is too tight. I try to bite him, but all that makes him do is clamp down on my mouth harder.

I feel like I can't breathe.

When he pumps his hips against me in the most vulgar way, I start to hyperventilate, certain he's going to either rape me or kill me, or both. The feeling of his body against mine makes my flesh crawl.

Roughly, a hand digs into my hair and yanks it back, and then he slams my face against my car one more time. I can taste blood in my mouth, and an agonizing pain splinters through me.

The metallic tang of blood on my tongue makes me feel nauseated. Dizzy. There is a gulf of blackness, and I force myself to stay conscious. I'm frightened. Scared. Weak. And I hate being weak. I focus on that. Using that rising anger to fight him off, anyway I can.

With all my might, I somehow manage to get my foot out of the vise-like lock his legs have my legs in, and donkey kick him right in the balls.

"Motherfucker," he sneers and takes ahold of my hair again, this time even harder, pulling me back away from the car.

I'm shaking from head to toe as fear curls in my belly, spreading to my chest and into my throat, grabbing me, and squeezing me until I can barely breathe. *He's going to kill me right now.*

When he lets go of me instead of inflicting more pain, my mind races with what to do.

Should I turn and gauge his eyes out?

Grab him by the balls?

Stomp on his foot and then run?

Or scream my brains out?

I'm calculating which move might work when he shoves something in my pocket and whispers, "Good luck, sweetheart."

His breath smells of coffee, and his cologne is vile, and a faint memory rips through me, making me stumble. I know who this is.

With a hard shove, he pushes me to the ground.

I fall in a heap, panic now all I know. I close my eyes tightly. I can't move. I can't breathe. My throat closes up when I try to scream. Somehow I manage to raise my hands to defend myself, but nothing happens. Slowly, I open my eyes and look up, expecting to see him pointing a gun at me or holding a knife, but he's gone.

Tears are stinging my eyes, making everything a blur. I stumble as I try to stand and end up crawling to the car and using it to make myself get up. I look around and see no one. I scream anyway. Scream and scream and scream.

My phone. I need my phone. My purse is on the ground and the contents have spilled. Searching, I spot it.

I'm breathing deeply, trying to slow my heart rate, to quell the panic still rising in my chest as I lurch for it.

But I can't stop it. I can't focus. I can't seem to find my feet. I stumble as I bend to get it, land on my hands and knees, and then crawl to it.

Bleeding and crying, I sit on the ground and call 911. Once I've explained what happened, I find my wallet and keys and start moving. Running, I head toward the café for safety. My fingers tremble as I try to put the key in the lock. It won't fit. The more I try to turn it, the more it keeps jamming.

Giving up, I hold my keys tightly in my hand. My tears are falling so hard I can barely see the blur through them. Sagging against the door, it's then that I realize the door is unlocked or the lock is jammed because it swings in.

In early morning dawn, I can't really see inside, but as soon as I step through the glass doors and turn the lights on, I can see there is no safety inside.

The place has been vandalized. Graffiti is strewn all over the walls. The paint and chemicals that were left behind have been opened and poured out all over the floors, and someone took a sledgehammer to the drywall. The place has been demolished.

Shaking beyond my control, I slide down the wall to the ground. I've felt alone many times in my life, but never more than right now. With my phone still in my hand, I call the only person I can.

She answers right away. "Tess, is everything okay?"

"No Fiona, no it isn't," I cry.

"What's wrong?"

I do my best to tell her.

She stays on the phone with me until the police arrive. It takes them more than ten minutes to get to the café, and less than ten minutes to write up their report. I tell them what I know. That my attacker was wearing a black ski mask that covered his face, and his body was also covered in black. The entire time I can hear my phone ringing from inside my purse. I assume it is Fiona, but I can't very well stop what I'm doing. I'll call her back once I'm finished.

"Anything else about his appearance you can tell us?"

I shake my head. "He never let me turn around."

In response they tell me there is not much they can do without more of a description. When I attempt to explain to them that his breath smelled, and that I've smelled that same vile coffee breath before, they stop me before I can say anymore. Facts, they only want facts, not hearsay or suspicions, they insist.

I'm holding a damp cloth to the side of my face when Ethan arrives. Since Fiona couldn't leave Max alone, or very well bring him, sending her husband to bring me to her house was the best solution. He gasps when he sees me, and once he makes sure I'm okay, he turns to yell at the officers for not having already arranged to have me transported to the emergency room. While Ethan reads them the riot act, Ash comes flying through the door.

I blink several times, not understanding what he's doing here. "Are you okay?" he asks. "Anything broken?"

I shake my head, no I'm not okay, and no nothing is broken, and then I can't stop a low whimper from stuttering past my stiff, swollen lips.

Seeing that I am shaken up, Ash enfolds me in his arms.

Hoarsely, I whisper in his ear, "It was Mathias Bigelow."

He pulls back and gently pushes the hair from my eyes. "How can you be sure?" he whispers.

"His breath."

Ash looks at me for a long time. "Did he say or do anything else?"

I nod, remembering the paper he shoved in my pocket. Slowly, I pull it out. It's the other help wanted sign that was taken from the café window on Friday. "He shoved this in my pocket, and said good luck, sweetheart."

Looking at it, he says, "I don't understand."

Before I can explain, the officers turn to address me. "Miss Winters, is there anything else you can tell us?"

Ash shakes his head, signaling for me to stay quiet.

"No, I've told you everything I can remember right now."

One of the officers hands me his card. "If you think of anything, please call me. Mr. Miller insists on transporting you to the emergency room, are you in agreement with this?"

I nod.

Once both officers are out the door and back in their car, Ash speaks up. "What am I missing, Tess?"

I walk over to the makeshift desk, which is oddly still standing, and pick up the other sign. I hand it to him, and then explain what happened on Friday.

His face goes white, and he pulls out his phone.

Ethan narrows his eyes at him. "What the hell is going on?"

Raising a finger in the air, Ash turns around to whisper into his phone.

"We need to get you to the hospital and get that cut stitched up," Ethan says, lifting and patting the cloth that I was holding to my face.

I suck in a breath, knowing that crying will only make the cut on my cheek burn more. "How did Ash find out what happened?" I ask Ethan.

Ethan daps at my face lightly. "I called Nick on my way here."

I wince from the pain spreading across the side of my face. "And he answered when you called?"

Ethan shakes his head. "I had to call Hayden and make him put the fucker on the phone."

I take the cloth from Ethan and press it against my face. "Did he say why he hasn't answered any of my calls?"

He nods. "He said he saw Ansel at your place Saturday night, down on one knee proposing to you."

My eyelids flutter as I try to figure out how I hadn't seen him.

"And the dumb fuck naturally thought you would say yes."

"Why would he think that?"

"Because he's a dumb fuck."

I almost laugh, but the pain that spreads across my lips stops me instantly. "Did you tell him I sent Ansel away?"

"Yeah, I did, and a few more things too."

"Did he believe you?"

Ethan motions toward Ash. I turn my head slowly and see he's holding his hand over the speaker of his phone. "Nick wants to talk to you. Are you up to it?"

I hold out my hand, and Ash brings me his phone. I walk toward the corner of the café and slowly sit on one of the only upright paint cans. Then I suck in a breath and say, "Hey."

"Tess," he breathes.

I take a long moment to compose myself.

"Tess, are you there?"

"I'm here," I whisper.

"I'm so sorry, baby. I'm at the airport now. I'll be in Chicago as soon as I can. I need to see you."

The agony in his voice can be heard so clearly that it makes me cry.

"Tess, listen to me, I shouldn't have left without talking to you. I just couldn't bear to lose you, and I thought I had. I really thought I had. I'm so sorry. I'm so sorry. Please tell me you forgive me."

My heart seizes in my chest and my tears burn as they stream down my face. I remember our conversation weeks ago, and I remember promising him that I would stand by him, no matter what. "Nick," I breathe.

"Tess, I love you."

I don't even hesitate. "I love you, too."

His voice is so hoarse I can barely hear him. "Listen to me, baby, I want you to stay with Ash until I get there. You're not to go anywhere without him. Do you understand me, Tess?"

I swipe at my tears and wince at the pain. "Yes, but Nick, what is going on?"

"I don't know yet, but we're going to figure everything out, I promise, but for now, I need to know that you're safe. Ash will take you to the hospital, and then back to my place. I'll be there as soon as I can."

"Okay," I answer, and then I feel everything inside me erupt into belly-deep sobs.

"Baby, please don't cry."

"Tell him you'll call him later," Ethan demands.

Before I can say anything though, Ash takes the phone from me, and I can hear him speaking to Nick, and then I feel Ethan's arms going around me and before I know it, he's carrying me across the café and out the door, into Ash's car.

Ash is behind the wheel, and he hangs up the phone. "I'll call you and Fi as soon as we're at Nick's apartment."

Ethan looks over at him. "I'd really rather you bring her to my house. Fiona is going to hit the roof."

Ash seems torn. "Look man, I don't think Tess is in any more danger, but I can't be sure."

"Yeah, you're right," Ethan says, and then gently kisses my head. "I'll talk to you soon, okay?"

I look up at him. "I'll call you and Fiona when I get settled."

Ethan closes my door, and I watch Ash as he waits for Ethan to get in his car before he drives away.

"What's going on?" I ask him.

Ash shakes his head.

"Please tell me. I think I have a right to know."

He sighs, and then looks over at me. "After Nick underbid Bigelow on the property he rented you, Bigelow started pulling the rug out from under us. And things have only escalated from there. The deal down in Miami is bad. It looks like the sale of the property is going to be frozen until the legality of the funds used can be determined."

"But Nick said he gave me a fair price for renting the property," I insist.

"Fair is subjective. Bigelow didn't see it that way, and so he took whatever deals he could from Nick. But Nick and Hayden didn't like the rug being pulled out from under them, and they slung it right back at him, tricking Bigelow into a property in Englewood."

Things are making more sense. "The one on Elizabeth Street?"

"Yes, the address that was written on your sign."

"But why did he attack me this morning?"

Ash looks over at me again. "To make it personal. Because he could. Who the fuck knows."

"Why didn't you want me to tell the police?"

"Because we can't be sure they're not on his payroll. It's better if Bigelow thinks you don't know what is going on."

"Better for me, you mean?"

He nods.

At that I turn and stare out the window, and only then to allow my eyes to close.

I've been a lot of things in my life, but I've never been this scared.

Thirty-Six

Nick

REGRET.

The word means different things to different people. It even means different things to the same person depending on the circumstances.

I regret not walking down the hallway of her apartment building Saturday night and fighting for what was mine. I regret making it look like I was blowing her off because I couldn't handle the rejection. But I don't regret for one single second allowing her in my life, forming an attachment, opening my heart enough to let her in.

I press the button for my floor, and then look over to Hayden, who is on the phone with his girlfriend.

"Alliecat, listen, I'm going to be fine. Just stay at your mother's until I come get you."

I run a hand down my face. Things have gotten way out of control.

Hayden scuffs the toe of his boot against the carpet in the elevator while she talks, then he softly says, "I love you too. Give munchkin a kiss for me. I'll be there as soon as I can."

After he hangs up, I look over at him. "She okay?"

He puts his hands in his pockets and leans back, looking just as exhausted as me. "She's fine. Just shaken up."

"When are you going to marry that girl?" I ask.

He lifts his gaze. "I don't know. Things are good the way they are, I don't want to rock the boat, you know?"

I nod, and we both fall silent.

It's been a rough couple of days.

The doors open and as soon as we step out, Ash storms toward us. "What the fuck is going on?"

Wanting to speak softly because Ash informed me when I landed that Tess was in my room asleep, I motion Ash and Hayden toward the kitchen.

Hayden speaks first. "We have a serious problem."

"No shit, Sherlock. What the hell happened to Tess?" Ash asks, thrusting the sign he already told me about at me. "Why is the property you had me scout out written on this?"

I take it and then stagger back to sit in one of the kitchen chairs. I bury my face in my hands and crumple the sign in my fist before I let it fall to the ground. After a moment, I look up. "Shut down all the deals you have going on. We're pulling our bid on Miami, backing down on all deals, and laying low."

Hayden's face is a mixture of shock and rage. "You're going to let him win?"

I blow out of breath. "Yeah, I am. Bigelow has people on his payroll all over the goddamned place. Even the FBI for Christ sake. If we continue to fight him, he's going to do something that ice and a few stitches can't cure, and I'm not willing to let that happen."

Hayden steps forward and snatches up the sign from the floor, stares at it, and sits down next me. "Hey, I'm on the same page. I am. I don't want anything to happen to anyone around us, but

Nick, if you let the Miami deal go, the Feds are going to hold your deposit indefinitely, and then if you squash all the deals we have in play right now, there will be no cash flow. This could ruin you."

I lean down and put my elbows on my knees. "And if I don't pull my bid, Bigelow is going to ruin all of us. One way or another, he's going to keep coming after us. Miami was just the first step. I mean how the hell did he manage to include my old man, the realtor's office, and the company in his set up?"

Hayden scratches his head. "I can't figure it out."

"And I doubt we ever will. Sure, if we fight him, we'll get out of the charges, eventually, but the company name will be smeared through the mud in the process. Men like Bigelow don't stop there. Tess is proof of that. He's going after me, then he'll go after you," I point to Hayden, "and then you," I point to Ash. "One by one until no one in the company is left standing." I look over to Hayden. "So yeah, we are standing the fuck down, no matter how much it kills me."

Ash brings me an icepack and motions with his chin toward my room. "She needs a new one."

I take it and stand, glancing at Hayden, who nods at me. "We'll get through this," I tell him. "I built the company from nothing once before, and if I have to, I'll do it again."

"Yeah, I know you will," he concedes.

"Don't get me wrong," I say, "I'm going to take Bigelow down, just not right now. I'm going to let him think he won, and then I'll find a way to ruin him. Legitimately. It can't be hard, there's a lot of real dirt on him out there. But mark my words, the day I find a way, is the day he turns up half-dead in a hospital bed for what he did to Tess."

Hayden looks up. "You're not going alone, man. I'll be right beside you."

Ash clamps a hand on both of our shoulders. "And I'll be right beside you both."

Eyes locked, the three of us share a look that says, *'The devil will get his due.'*

And that is one promise I will never regret.

Thirty-Seven

Nick

I WAS AN asshole.

Fuck, I am an asshole.

That's the only thing I can think about as I stand above her.

No amount of discussions and descriptions can prepare a man to see the woman he loves banged up and bruised. Ash had told me one side of her face was swollen, and the gash on her cheek had to have five stitches to be closed back up, but motherfucker, the rage that boils inside me as I stare down at her is enough to drive me to act immediately. To kill Bigelow and put this whole issue to rest right now.

Except where would that leave me, but in a ten by ten cell for the rest of my life. And then he'd still fucking win.

Even though it kills me to know she's laying here like this because of me, what I did to him, I will wait and strike when the time is right.

In the meantime, I have a lot of making up to do to this woman, and if I have to spend my whole life doing it, I'll gladly do so.

I want her with me, always. The thought should scare the shit out of me, but instead it tells me what I have to do. What I think I always wanted to do from the moment I first set eyes on her more than three years ago. I'm going to marry her.

Feeling whole maybe for the first time in my life, I reach a hand out to stroke her face, staying clear of the dark purple bruising that looks so vivid against her pale skin.

Sitting beside her, I smooth her hair back and then lean down to brush my lips across hers. "I love you," I murmur.

One side of her mouth tips up, and then her beautiful eyes flutter open. "You're here," she whispers.

Kicking my shoes off, I lie down beside her, and again brush my lips lightly against hers. "I'm here, just like I said I would be. And I promise you that I won't leave you again, ever, no matter what."

A small sigh escapes her swollen lips. "You're very confident that I'm going to let you back in life."

Her voice is small and quiet, and although she's trying to make light of my ill actions, her words cut me deep in my soul.

Reaching my hand out, I smooth it down the t-shirt of mine she's wearing to find her small hand. I take it and lace our fingers together. "Please, Tess, tell me you forgive me."

Tess is in the middle of the bed, and she reaches across the space to put her hand on my shoulder and urge me closer.

I go, my head moving to her pillow, only inches away from hers.

Tears well in her eyes. "I'm sorry you had to see that," she says softly. "I had no idea Ansel was coming to Chicago. I would have never let him come to see me had I known. Do you believe me?"

Gently, I take her face in my hands, careful not to exude any pressure to the left side, and wipe her tears away. "Oh, baby," I say in an aching voice. "Don't cry. And don't apologize. You have nothing to be sorry for. This was my fault. My ghosts. And it's time I grow up and face them."

She takes my hands and brings them to her mouth, kissing them, and then urges me closer still. "I'm not going anywhere."

"I know."

"I'm not going to leave you for someone else."

"I know."

"Good. Now kiss me," she says, "and then tell me again that you love me, this time so I can see your face when you do."

That's one order I'm more than happy to follow.

Thirty-Eight

Nick

LATER THAT NIGHT when everyone has gone, I sit beside her while she sleeps and look out at the Chicago skyline.

The lights twinkle and gleam.

Life has a way of presenting itself, and when it does, it's best to grab it by the horns and just ride along rather than trying to fight it every step of the way.

And that's what I decided to do.

This woman was handmade for me. When I'm with her, there are no constraints like attachment or commitment, because those seemed to have evolved naturally.

She has become my world.

Everything I never knew I wanted, but everything I need, and I'm not going to fight it.

Tess had spent the day in bed, but by five, she was ready to move around. Fiona came over and brought her some clothes and dinner. After we ate, Ash hung around so I could run out and do something I couldn't wait to do any longer. By the time I'd gotten back, Tess had fallen asleep on the couch and Fiona had left. I thanked Ash, and he too went home.

It's close to eight now, and Tess is just waking up. I've been watching her sleep, and thinking about life, and what I want from it. The answer is so clear—it is her.

When her eyes flutter open, I stand up and offer her my hand. "Join me outside by the fire," I say.

She grins and gives me her hand. "Why Nick Carrington, are you trying to seduce me?"

Gently, I help her to her feet, careful to make sure the bruise on her stomach doesn't cause her too much pain. "Baby, I've told you over and over, I don't need game, my charm wins the ladies over every time."

She wraps her arms around me and tugs me close to her. "Your charm might have worked in the past, but this lady expects both romance and charm."

I look into her eyes. "Come with me, I have something for you."

She pushes back slightly and starts patting me down. "Please don't ruin the moment with another box of lubricant," she laughs.

I shake my head. "Am I ever going to be able to live that down?"

"Never," she grins.

Outside, we sit by the fire and talk. She tells me about Ansel, and her attack, and her deep sorrow that the café has been vandalized. I listen and reassure her that we will make her dream come true, but for now, I tell her, "I think we should leave that property alone." Then I tell her what has happened with Carrington Development, and how Bigelow is gunning for us.

"This all started because I didn't rent from him," she sighs.

I shake my head. "This all started because I went to war with him, not because of you."

She stares at me. "What's going to happen?"

I look around. "I'm not sure. I'm going to have to sell this place to keep the company on its feet."

"What? Why?"

"With so much of the company money tied up in Miami, if I don't, it won't be long before we won't be able to meet our monthly obligational needs."

"But you love this place."

I hadn't planned a way to do this because I knew I would never follow it. But now seems like the perfect time, so I drop to one knee in front of her. "And I'll love my new place even more, especially if you agree to make it ours."

Her eyes widen in surprise.

And then I reach into my pocket and pull the small velvet box from it. "I love you, baby, and I wanted to do this in the perfect moment, but I can't wait." I flip the box open to show her the perfect round diamond that sparkles just like her. "Marry me. I know we haven't been together long, but I've wanted this from the moment we met. I just didn't know it, but you showed me the way. So Tess, say yes, and make me the happiest man in the world. Tell me you'll be mine."

She is shaking and her hands are trembling, and at first I'm not sure what she's thinking as the tears stream down her cheeks. But then she offers me her left hand and says, "Yes. Nick, yes! I'll marry you. I love you so much."

Once I slide the ring on her finger, I smile and push myself up so I can gather her in my arms, and then I kiss her as gently as I can.

This woman has become a part of me I never knew was missing and I don't plan to ever be without her.

Minutes later we're in bed and I'm holding her tight. "I have a confession," I tell her.

She looks up at me. "Is it something bad?"

I toss her a rueful grin. "No, baby, it's not. Remember when you asked me if I wanted you to be my baby momma?"

With a smile of her own, she cups my check with her left hand, her ring sparkling on her finger in the dim light. "There are so many things I could say right now, but I think I'll go easy on you and just say yes."

I slide my lips to her hand and kiss it. "Thank you, I really appreciate that."

"Oh, there's no need to thank me. I expect something in return, but I'll save my request until you tell me why you're asking."

I shake my head. Even slightly battered and bruised, her sass is still there. "What if I told you I wanted to say yes, when you asked me that?"

She rises onto her elbow. "You mean you want to get me pregnant on purpose?"

I kiss her on the lips. "Yeah, I do, but only after I marry you."

Seriousness crosses her brow. "But you just said you're going to be homeless, and there's no way we can live in my small place."

A deep belly laugh escapes my throat. "Oh, baby, I'm going to buy us a house, and hopefully have you pregnant by the first day of summer."

Her beautiful eyes stare at me in wonder.

I run my finger along the bandage on he cheek. "Tess, I will always take care of you. I'm going to sell this place because what I'll get for it will be enough to buy a house and float the business."

"Do you think we could find something close to Fiona and Ethan?"

I give her a smile. "Is that what you want?"

She nods.

"Then I know we can. So is that yes?"

She nods again. "Yes, I'll have your babies."

"Babies?"

"I want four kids."

"Four?" I pretend to be in shock, but secretly I was thinking more like six.

She gingerly moves her body so she's lying on top of me.

"What are you doing?"

With a press of her hips to mine, she purrs. "Getting started on our family."

I shake my head. "Baby, we shouldn't. You have to take it easy."

She presses her mouth lightly to my neck. "Then we'll take it easy, and slow."

I groan and thrust my hips upward. "Are you sure you're up for it?"

Her hand glides down and finds my cock, already getting hard. "This is what I want for being a good girl earlier."

I smile and drag my fingers up the skimpy camisole she'd changed into before getting into bed. It didn't go unnoticed that she was only wearing that and her panties when she slipped in bed.

I, on the other hand, opted not to sleep naked like I always do, and to keep my boxers on, to ensure I would be a good boy.

Guess even good boys turn out to be bad.

Once I have the hem of her top in my fingertips, I push it up. "You were a very good girl, and I think you deserve whatever you want for that. Tell me," I whisper, my fingers gliding up the sides of her breasts. "What do you want?"

"Do I get anything?"

"Always."

Tess slowly moves off of me and sits against the headboard with her legs spread wide. Her top is halfway up her body, where I left it.

I watch her, my breath catching at the vision before me.

"I want you to love me."

I look at her and see the same desire in her eyes that is flowing through my veins. Unable to deny her, I strip my boxers off and crawl down the bed. "Always," I whisper, as I place a kiss on each of her ankles. "Forever," I say nuzzling her knees, one then the other.

"Until the day I die," I moan, licking up the inside of her thigh.

Her fingers trail over my body, soft and sensual, with every move I make.

I map out her body, each beautiful inch of it. The inside of her elbows, the tips of her fingers, the long column of her neck, the slope of her breasts, the curve of her hips, the dip of her belly button.

Only once my mouth has grazed every square inch of the front of her body, do I cup her face against mine where I feel the flutter of her lashes against my skin, and whisper, "I love you. You're mine. I'm yours. We belong to each other, forever."

"Forever," she whispers.

And then slowly, softly, and gently, I remove her clothes and very carefully roll her onto her stomach, where I kiss each of her shoulder blades, lick down her spine, kiss the backs of her legs, her calves, and her ankles again.

Trailing my tongue back up one of her thighs, I stop before I reach her sex, and then gently roll her over so that I can stare down at her. "You're beautiful."

She takes my face in her hands and says, "I love you."

With her words all I can hear, I slide into her, and move so slow that it takes us each a very long to climax. When we do finally tip into orgasm, her name is on my lips, my name is on hers, and I can feel the love between us, unlike I've felt anything in my life.

And it feels really, fucking great!

Epilogue

Tess

THIS FOURTH OF July when Nick moons me, there's no doubt that I'm his intended target because he pulls his shorts all the way down, making sure I see every inch of his fine ass.

And see I do.

Breathing hard, I lick my lips a little, and my heart skips a beat.

Seriously, his ass is so tight. So hot. I shove the lemons aside and wipe my hands, just so I can gawk.

"Well," he says over his shoulder.

"Your ass looks very fine, sweetheart," I giggle, circling the island to get a closer view.

"You know I'm not talking about my ass," he grumbles.

I pucker my lips. "I'm sorry?" I suggest.

Then with a sigh, he turns around to show me his very erect cock. "Sorry! That doesn't work, baby."

I shrug. "I was just trying to have a little fun. You looked so serious sitting at your desk."

"I was working, and this," he points down to his penis that is now jutting straight out, "is what you," he points to my bikini, "did to me up there with your lap dance."

"Oh my." I cover my mouth. "What are you going to do about that? Everyone will be here in an hour, and although you are always the life of the party, I don't think our guests will appreciate you walking around looking like the hotdogs are in your shorts."

Nick steps out of his shorts and strides toward me. "You're hilarious."

Feeling playful, I shimmy my bottoms down and let them fall to the floor. Then I run a finger down my stomach and around my clit. "Is this what you want?"

His dark gaze darts to my pussy. "You know it is."

"Ask me what I want?"

He narrows his eyes. "This isn't a negotiation."

I hop up on the counter with my legs spread wide and start to play with myself. "Oh, this feels so good."

"Tess, it isn't funny. We're having company in less than an hour, we don't have time for your games."

I throw my head back and continue circling my clit. "But you love it when I play games."

He's inbetween my legs now, his gaze so heavy with desire, that I almost give in, but this is way too fun. "Yes, I do, when we have time. Right now we don't have time."

I lift my finger and swipe it over his lips. "I can make myself come in less than three minutes. I'll even let you watch. See, I have plenty of time."

He licks at my finger, greedy-like. "Okay, what do you want?"

I remove my finger from his mouth and cross my legs. "I want to watch you make yourself come."

He shakes his head no. He still refuses to do that one thing for me. "I don't get why that fascinates you. If I needed to jerk off, why would you be there? It makes no sense."

"You've watched me make myself come."

"Yeah, because it's hot."

"See."

He just stares at me.

I uncross my legs and continue circling. "Oh, yes, this feels so good."

"Fine," he mutters, and moves his hand to cup my pussy.

I push it away. Tsk. Tsk. "Tonight, after the party?"

"Yes, after the party I'll put on a porn show."

"You promise?"

"I promise."

I give him a smug smile.

"You're such a dirty girl," he growls.

I untie my top and let it fall to the ground. "Good thing that's how you like me. Now let's take care of your little problem. See how easy it is when you just play along."

He shakes his head at me. "You've been a very bad girl. If we had time, there are so many things I'd do to that sassy mouth. But I'll have to save those things for later. Now stand up and turn around. And I don't want you to come until I say so. This is for me."

I never knew how good being bad could be—until him.

I turn around and bend over, so wet for him that I swear I am dripping down my leg. He shows no mercy when he thrusts deep inside me. I gasp, loving the feeling. Loving that we can make love or fuck, and sometimes do a little of both. We've determined we're both living the horny teenager years we never got to experience. Him because he was taking care of his brother, and me because I was trying to do what my parents wanted.

Now we do what we want, when we want.

As he pumps into me, I look around our kitchen, at the bright white cabinets and pale yellow walls, the dark hardwood floors, and the marble countertops, and then I glance at the diamond ring and wedding band on my finger. I still can't believe I get to spend the rest of my life with this man.

True to his word, Nick married me and bought us a house in Lincoln Park, both before the first day of summer. The house is one we picked out together. It's a four-bedroom, two-story house with a huge backyard, a swimming pool, and a basketball court, of course. In truth, I'm pretty sure that is what sold him on the house. What sold me was the white picket fence, and the hope of a life I never even dreamed of.

We got married in a church because I knew it would make my parents happy. It was a small ceremony, and we threw a huge party afterwards at the same place Ethan and Fiona held their engagement party. Nick says it's where he fell in love with me, and that celebrating our marriage there would bring us full circle.

How could I argue with that?

Nick's thrusts become faster, and he goes deeper, and I want to come, I want to come so badly, I can't help but moan. "Don't you dare," he whispers in my ear. "Not until I say."

I hold back, and I can feel how close he is, but even as he comes, calling out my name, he says nothing to me.

My punishment.

Don't worry, what comes around goes around with us—always.

When he sags into me, he bites my shoulder, and then he places one hand on my belly. I'm six weeks pregnant, and although we should wait to tell everyone, we're too excited not to tell them today.

I moan again, the pain of the impending pleasure almost too much to bear.

Giving in to me, his hand goes to my clit. "You were a very good girl for waiting. Do you want to come?"

"Yes, sir, yes I do."

He groans with excitement whenever I say sir. And I know when I do, I always get my way.

As predicted, he makes his move. His hand slides up from my belly to my breast and he pinches my nipple. "Who owns this body?"

"You," I purr.

With satisfaction, he inserts a finger inside me while his thumb circles me with just the right amount of pressure. "Who do you come for?" he asks.

"You," I moan.

"Who always makes you feel good?"

"You," I cry, moaning and twisting.

"There you go, baby, now come for me."

And come I do, calling out his name over and over. I like to play games before sex, he likes to play them during sex. It couldn't be more perfect.

Having worked himself back up, he whirls me around and crashes his lips to mine, sliding his tongue in to taste me.

When he pulls away, he inserts the tip of his cock only slightly into my pussy. For several long seconds, he plays, pushing in and out, going a bit deeper with each thrust.

I look down, enjoying the sight of his cock sliding from my pussy, wet and slick.

"You like that?" he whispers, thrusting hard and deep.

"Yes," I breathe, running my hands down his hard abs.

"You're so tight. So snug."

I moan softly, and he pauses, withdrawing and then pushing forward in slow fucking motions. "Tell me what you like," he says, looking down now too, watching the sliding motion of his cock in and out of my pussy.

I lean against the counter to get a better view. "Your cock inside me."

He pushes in harder. "Where inside you?" he grounds out.

My body is spiraling as he continues to work me. "In my pussy, in my mouth, and in my ass."

I can't help it, I'm a dirty, dirty girl.

Harder, deeper, he moves. His hips smack against mine and I cry out, my pussy convulsing around him.

"Oh, fuck, Tess, that's it," he groans.

My cry nearly splinters the room, as this time we both come together.

He closes his eyes, and then sags against me. "You undo me, Tess, " he murmurs.

I sag against him. "You undo me, too," I murmur back.

And once we've regained our strength, we head upstairs to shower and get ready for the party we're throwing. We might live in a constant state of being undone, but for now it is time to do ourselves up, if only for a little while.

Later that night, once the fireworks have gone off and all the hotdogs and hamburgers have been eaten, I stand on the back deck with Nick's arms wrapped around me and look around at all the people in our life.

Fiona, Ethan, and Jace are sitting together around the bonfire. Their threesome thing is over, but nothing between them seems to have changed. Fiona ended it, although she did so in that way that made it seem like it was mutual.

First, she suggested to Jace that he move Scarlett to The Preston School this fall and because it is the best around, he decided to. After he registered Scarlett, Fiona insisted Jace meet Max's teacher, who will be Scarlett's teacher next year. You remember, Miss Eastling, the pretty one who wears her hair in a chignon. And believe it or not, Fiona's matchmaking skills might have worked this time. Jace and Miss Eastling have a date next week.

When I asked Fiona why she ended things, all she said was Jace was ready to have someone in his life that he doesn't have to share.

Then I asked her what that meant for her and Ethan, and she told me that they were going to be just fine.

And I have no doubt they will be.

Shifting my gaze, it lands on Hayden, his girlfriend, and Ash, who are sitting by the pool with their feet dangling in the water. Hayden finally asked Allie to marry him last week, but they aren't getting hitched until next summer.

Ash, on the other hand, says he's not ready to fall in love. There's still too much for him to do before he gets weighted down with the old ball and chain. His words, not mine.

The café is still on hold, and it might be that way for quite a while. Right now though, I'm content being Nick's wife, lover, and soon-to-be mother of his child. I never thought that would be what I wanted out of life—but it turns out it might be just what I needed to finally feel like me.

Nick says, "Don't be mad," and then lets go of me.

I turn to give him a confused look, but before I even fully turn around, he's streaking down the deck, running toward the pool, and jumping off the diving board, yelling, "Cannonball," as he moons our guests.

All I can do is shake my head.

I told you he always has to be the life of the party.

So yeah, as for the big kid known as Nick Carrington, his business took a huge lose last quarter, but now that he is back in the game, it is finally getting back on track.

Oh right, I almost forgot, as for Bigelow, he was arrested last month on three separate counts of tax evasion. If he is convicted, he will spend fifteen years in jail. Ethan is certain he will be convicted. In truth, I'm pretty certain he helped uncover the felony. Also, the same day Bigelow was charged and released on bail, three men in ski masks attacked him on his way home. His injuries weren't severe, but warranted that he spend the night in the hospital.

I didn't have to ask Nick if it was him.

I knew it was.

Just as I knew he did it for me.

And if it makes me a bad person to say Bigelow got what he deserved, then I'll make up for it in some good way someday.

It might be a warped sense of thinking, but I don't care.

The truth is—I'm different.

Nick's different.

We're all different.

And for the first time in my life, different doesn't feel bad.

In fact, it feels really good.

THE END

Look for . . .

Big Shot

(Jace's story) coming August 2017

Jace Bennett was the type of man you would love forever. Tall, dark, and brooding, there was just something about him that drew you in and captured your heart. It might have been that slow, sexy smile or his filthy, dirty mouth. Or it might have just been him.

What I didn't know back then was that although I'd love him forever, I wouldn't be the one sharing his bed, the one having his children, or the one he adored.

But then—that was because of me—not him.

AND

Hot Stuff

(Lucas's story) coming by the end of 2017

Lucas Carrington thinks he's hot stuff, both on and off the field.

Not that he isn't. Rough, tough, and sexy, the guy knows how to move, in every way.

The problem is just that—he knows it.

Someone needs to teach him a thing or two, and I think I'm just the one to do it.

About

Big Shot:

On the heels of Sexy Jerk comes a story that will steal your breath. Big Shot is filled with both humor and tears. Although this second chance romance is set in the Sexy Jerk world, it is a complete stand-alone.

Ten years ago I had no idea what I wanted out of life, until I met Hannah Michaels. She was a computer-engineering student ready to conquer the social media world, and I was smitten. Even though I knew she was taken, I had to have her.

Being the rich, moody bad boy that I was, I didn't let her status stand in my way. It wasn't long before my hands were on her thighs and my name a whisper on her lips. Soon after, we became inseparable, and she taught me so much. But as was the case with most things in my life at that time, I was more concerned with my own needs than the consequences of my actions. Before I could figure that out, she called me a *Big Shot*, and left.

I always wondered what happened to her, but I never found the courage to find out. Instead, I went on with my life, carrying a little piece of her with me every step of the way.

Having learned how to love from Hannah, I got married and had a daughter. My life was nearly perfect, but then my wife died, and my world turned upside down.

A single father has challenges, and one of those is learning how to calmly deal with your child coming home from school in tears. I had no idea the day I pounded on my daughter's classmate's door, Hannah would be the one standing on the other side.

Hannah didn't appreciate my tirade, and once again she called me a *Big Shot*. It shouldn't have turned me on. It shouldn't have reminded me of the sexual connection we once shared. And it definitely shouldn't have stirred up old feelings.

Irritated with myself, I left her standing there trying to convince me her son was not the bully I had accused him of being.

She didn't take kindly to that, and the next day, she was the one pounding on my door. The back and forth continued for over a month until we both couldn't stand the nearly combustible tension between us, and finally gave in to our all-consuming passion.

Guilt hit me like a hammer. I hated myself. I hated her. The problem was I really didn't hate her—I wanted her more than ever.

But this time around, I can't have her.

Not unless I can convince myself that just because I still have feelings for Hannah, that doesn't mean I loved my wife any less.

This time it's my status that stands in our way—and going up against myself just might be the hardest thing I've ever done.

And Now a Sneak Peek into

Hot Shot

"DADDY, WHAT ARE you doing?"

I looked up and blinked, and then blinked again. The sun was just rising and my daughter was standing in the space between my bedroom and bathroom in her pink nightgown. I squeezed my palm shut, and jumped to my feet. "I was just thinking."

"About what?" she asked with that voice of concern that made her sound ten years older than she was.

Honesty was always the best policy, when possible. "That we should donate Mommy's things to that organization Aunt Fiona works with."

She brought her hands together. "Oh, Daddy, I think that's a wonderful idea. Aunt Fiona says there a lot of mommies who need new clothes to go back to work."

I grinned at her innate kindness. "And what are you doing up this early, princess?"

Her tiny shoulders shrugged. "I woke up, and was thinking maybe you could put my hair in braids today."

Taking long strides toward her, I had her up in my arms and on my shoulders before she even finished talking. "You just happened to wake up early and have that thought, did you now?"

My daughter giggled as I galloped toward my bed and tossed her on it. Once her fit of laughter subsided, she sat up. "Well, I might have set my alarm the way you showed me so that I'd wake up early."

The clock read six twenty-five. Normally I didn't wake her up until seven to get her ready, and we were both downstairs by seven thirty when Mrs. Sherman arrived. "Wow," I said, offering her my hand, "you're a quick learner."

Her little bare toes landed on the plush area rug, and she looked up at me with wide green eyes. "You are too, Daddy, and I'm certain after that you-tube video we watched over the summer that you'll be able to braid my hair just like Polly showed you."

Polly was the you-tuber who made a show of explaining to fathers how to do all kinds of things with their daughters' hair, including braiding.

This was going to be one interesting morning.

I led Scarlett to her bathroom. "First you have to brush your teeth, and then get dressed. Once you finish that, I will try to braid you hair, but I make no promises," I said with a wink.

In the doorway, where the print of tiaras covered the walls, she stopped and attempted to comb her fingers through her tangled locks. "You're the best."

I smiled at her and kissed the top of her head. I only hoped she still thought that after I was finished—with the hair brushing and the braiding.

Chances were good that I wasn't going to get the results the you-tuber demonstrated.

Isn't that always the way.

And Also a Look into

No Pants Required

Chapter 1
She's a Very Kinky Girl

Makayla

JUST THE MERE suggestion of karaoke gets everyone's heart pounding. Whether it's out of excitement or pure, blind panic depends on the individual and that person's frame of mind at the time.

The truth is that most people sing karaoke for the same reasons they go bowling—it's a fun activity and they can drink while doing it.

With that being said, perhaps some of the people that are here can get up and confidently belt out their most favorite song in the world with no concern for the cardrums they are perforating or the notes they are destroying. Unfortunately, I am not one of those people.

To be honest, I can't believe I even agreed to do this.

Then again, Bar On is not where I thought I'd find myself tonight. This Chinatown lounge may be packed full of eager-to-sing regulars, but my friends and I are not those people. We are here on a whim after a few too many drinks at a restaurant down the street.

Shuffling through the crowd, I stop when someone taps me on the shoulder. Thinking it's one of my friends, I turn around to see a tall, leggy brunette with the most vibrant green eyes staring at me. Her face is stunning. She looks like Megan Fox. For a second, I wonder if she is.

She steps closer and right away I can see this woman is a bit younger, though—my age, I'd say. "Do you mind if I get by?" she asks with one of those affluent tones I know all too well from my days in private school.

Definitely not Megan Fox.

Without waiting for me to answer, she pushes past, and in her rush, steps on my open-toed pump.

Ouch!

I glare as her red Louboutin soles make their way to the front of the lounge.

"Come on," my coworker tosses over her shoulder, not at all bothered by the woman who brushed past her, too. "Sandra found us a table."

India leads the way, and I follow, making sure not to step on any toes in the crowd. Finally, she stops at the only available table large enough for our group, which just so happens to be right in front of the stage.

Fantastic.

The white leather banquette is awash in the neon light emanating from the human-sized letters that spell the establishment's name across the back wall. The light is nearly blinding. I look at Sandra. "Are you sure you want to sit this close?"

She hands me a menu of songs. "Yes, this is going to be great."

"Pour Some Sugar on Me" is coming to an end and once I've slid all the way across the bench, I look up to see a group of very pleased guys jumping off the stage in unison. The Def Leppard wannabes are staring at us.

This must have been their spot.

All clean-cut, all fuck-hot, all about my age. Immediately, I can tell by their walk that they are definitely Upper East Siders. Prep school, riot club types turned Wall Street wolves would be my guess. You know—the kind of guy your mother warns you about.

The type I should have stayed away from.

The guy closest to me is wearing a red tie and has his black jacket slung over his shoulder. The others are dressed in dark suits too. *Hmmm* . . . either dressed up for an occasion or still dressed up after the occasion. Not a wedding, since it's a Thursday night. An office party maybe? Or perhaps this group of drunken men is here for a going-away party like mine. Who knows? Anyway, the guy with the red tie gives the eight of us girls a quick glance and a smile but doesn't stop.

He's cute. Really cute.

At least he doesn't seem to mind that we took their table. Then again, he's too focused on the guy without a jacket farthest away from me. "Cam," he calls out. "Don't bother with her." His warning is too late, though, because this Cam, whose white, rumpled shirt and dark hair are all I can see, is already allowing himself to be dragged away from his group by that Megan Fox look-alike who practically ran me over minutes ago.

Fascinated by her assertiveness, I watch the two of them. I have to crane my neck to catch sight of them, and soon, too soon, they disappear into the crowd. Squinting my eyes, wishing I'd changed my dirty contact lenses, I search for them.

In a matter of seconds, though, it's not my poor eyesight but Sandra who prevents me from locating them. She stands in front of me with a huge-ass smile on her face. "What song did you decide on?"

Giving a cursory glance at my choices, the perfect one is the first I see. "'Total Eclipse of the Heart,'" I blurt out and point excitedly at the same time. This song I know, and know it all too well.

Sandra is my neighbor and is more than aware of all my woes. That sad smile she gives me borders on pity.

Not wanting to be *that girl* anymore, the one who got her heart broken, I grab Sandra's arm before she heads toward the karaoke booth. "You know what, forget that song. Why don't you pick one that represents the change coming in my life?"

At that her eyes light up.

Minutes later I'm being dragged up onstage by my friends and coworkers, and according to the screen, I'm about to sing a group rendition of "New York, New York."

Okay, I can do this.

I know this song. Not as well as "Total Eclipse of the Heart," but at least I know it. Besides, how hard can it be? I've sung it a million times—although admittedly mostly when I've been drunk.

Then again, I have had a lot to drink tonight.

The pressure is on. The eight of us gather around the microphone. The audience lights dim and a spotlight shines on us. I kind of feel like a star. No, I feel like Frank Sinatra himself without those penetrating blue eyes. But when the karaoke jockey asks, "Are you ready?" suddenly, I'm petrified. There is no way on God's green earth I am going to be able to hit the high notes.

The music starts. It's too late to back out. First, it's just the piano, but then the trumpet and clarinet join in. It's odd, but the familiarity of the sound eases my nerves. When the lyrics flash in front of me, all my worries are gone and I don't care anymore.

I let all of my hang-ups go and sing.

This, what I'm doing right now, is a glimpse into the old me. Somewhere between college and the real world, I lost that fun-loving girl, and I hope I can find her again.

Don't worry. I have a plan to do just that. Not only am I leaving the city I have loved for so long, but I'm also going to be moving far, far away, with no idea if I will ever be coming back.

It's how I hope to find myself.

My friends squeeze my shoulders, and we continue to sing the lyrics. Unexpectedly, they alter the words, and instead of talking about making it in New York, they tell the story of making it anywhere—in my case, California.

More than moved by this kind gesture, I gulp down the sorrow and move with them in a way that doesn't match the tempo at all. It doesn't matter, though, because they're right: "If I can make it here, I can make it anywhere."

God, I hope that's true.

There's a pause in the chorus and the piano melody quiets us all down. We're now standing in a straight line onstage and swaying back and forth.

Breathing for the first time in three months, *regret* isn't a word I am going to allow myself to say . . . out loud, anyway.

Yes, I admit it—I have a type A personality, which makes me hard to get to know and even harder to be friends with. Crossing my *t*'s and dotting my *i*'s will always be important to me. As is staying on a schedule. Making lists. And being organized. But none of that means I'm boring.

The sting of the word still hurts.

Sebastian was wrong. *Is* wrong—I am not boring, and even though he is out of my life I am going to prove him wrong. No, scratch that—I am going to prove to myself that I can live my life wild and free, because truth be told, I may not be boring, but I am bored.

I need a change.

To find myself.

The chorus starts up again and although we sing about coming to New York, we all do so knowing that I'm leaving.

I still can't believe I'm doing it.

When my best friend, Maggie, suggested on the phone, "Why don't you quit your job and move out here with me?" I nearly broke out in hives.

I thought, *why would I do that?*

My life was settled. I had a good job, an apartment, and a fiancé.

Then I remembered that my boss was an ass, my apartment was a sublet, and my fiancé, well, he wasn't mine anymore.

Once I let the idea of moving sink in, I thought, *why not make a new start?* At twenty-four and a half, I can afford to make a change. I'll get a new job. Give myself a year. Who knows, maybe even find myself.

I have nothing to lose.

If Laguna Beach isn't the place for me, then I'll come back to New York. And if I have to, I'll grovel to get back my old job at the fashion house. My soon-to-be-former boss might be an ass, but he knows my value to the company as a designer.

Completely oblivious to how this song ends, I mumble through it, laughing the entire time. When it's over, I'm the first to stumble off the stage. Soon after, my friends follow, and we all huddle together. The group of boys our mothers warned us about have reoccupied their seats, leaving us homeless.

"Let's sing another one," India suggests, practically jumping at the idea. India is—no, as of today, was—my coworker at Kate von Frantzenberg. We've been friends since we both started there right out of college. She's married to a great guy named Elvis—yes, Elvis. And she, like Sandra, saw me through the dark times following my breakup with Sebastian.

Another song does seem like fun. Karaoke is addicting. However, my bladder is about to burst. "You guys go for it," I tell her. "I'm going to use the bathroom and I'll hop in when I'm done."

"Stay out of trouble," she calls to me.

"Don't worry, I'll be good," I tell her and weave my way through the crowd toward the restrooms.

Trouble.

That's a laugh.

Even if I went looking for it, it would never find me.

Boring.

My life is that boring.

Wonder of wonders, there is only a very short line. Gleeful and relieved when I finally push through the bathroom door, I hurry to find an empty stall. The hard part comes next. My dress is tight, too tight to shimmy over my hips. With its large silver zipper running up the entire back, I have to use both hands to get it down. Getting it back up is just as much of a bother.

An episode of *Sex and the City* comes to mind. One in which Carrie Bradshaw finally accepts being alone and figures out how to zip her own dress.

If she could do it, so can I.

Channeling my inner Carrie, it still takes me a few minutes. And when I come out of the stall, the bathroom is jam-packed. I wait my turn for a sink behind two women whispering loudly about the tragedy of it all and how they don't blame him for leaving the city. *Him.* I don't know who they are talking about, but by the time the two women leave, even I feel sorry for this *him.*

After I wash my hands and dry them, I follow the surge of people down the dimly lit hallway. There are rooms reserved for private parties and with my feet killing me, I slip into an empty one to check my messages.

Strips of neon-pink bulbs along the perimeter cast an almost strobe-like effect in the room. Ignoring the fact that it's messing with my vision, I pick a booth out of sight of the door. My screen saver lights up when I pull my phone from my purse. It's of the Statue of Liberty. A photo I took last summer when Sebastian and I were goofing off one Saturday instead of looking for wedding locations.

I should have taken it as a sign.

Resolved to stop thinking about Sebastian, I thumb across the picture and go directly to Google. Once there, I search for a picture of something that will have meaning in my new life.

Bingo!

More than satisfied with my choice, I save it as my new screen saver and start singing the song that the bright photo reminds of: "If you like piña coladas . . ."

With a smile on my face, I finish that verse and flip to my message. When I do, I see that I have a text.

Maggie: Are you still out?

Feeling on top of the world that yes, I am, I look at the time and smile. It's 12:35 a.m. And I'm still out. Having fun.

See, I'm so not boring.

Excited about this, I have to retype my reply three times to get the one word correct. Just as I go to hit send, my phone slides out of my grip.

Crap.

Camouflaged beneath the black tablecloth, I lie on the seat and reach onto the carpeted floor. The smoothness of the vinyl bench and soft material of my dress don't exactly see eye-to-eye, and somehow I end up falling to the ground. It's more than a little grimy and I'm more than a little grossed out. With my fingers curled around my phone, I'm about to get off this disgustingness when I hear the sound of voices and the door closing to the private room.

I freeze right where I am.

From under the table I can see two silhouettes. A man. And a woman. I can't see their faces from this angle, only their bodies. Just as I'm about to announce my presence, my eyes drift down to a perfectly shined pair of men's shoes and a very familiar pair of high heels. I know by the Louboutins that the woman is the Megan Fox look-alike.

Like a cat, my curiosity is back.

And when she shoves the man against the door, I feel my heart start to pound. The man is likely Cam—the dark-haired guy she trampled over me to get to and then dragged away from his friends.

Getting a better look at him, I can see that his body is taut with tension. A live wire, I think. Definitely an uptight suit.

Trust me—I know the type well.

Right now is when I should announce myself. Yet I don't. Instead, I cover the screen of my phone to shield its glare and watch for what she's going to do next. Maybe yell at him. Cry. Or even break up with him. She's a woman on a mission, and I feel an odd kinship with her because I've been there before.

As if releasing her rage, she rips his shirt apart, and I panic as the buttons jump across the carpeted floor and land very close to my table. The couple doesn't even seem to notice, though, because the woman is already running her palms up his smooth, muscled skin. When she bends, I think for a moment she might bite him or pinch him, and then tell him to go to hell, but instead she starts licking him.

Wait!

She was mad at him.

Wasn't she?

Had I gotten her body language all wrong?

From my downtown view, I can tell she's working his one nipple hard. His hands claw at the door behind him as if he needs the support, but his satisfied groans tell me he likes what's going on. When Megan moves to the other side of his chest, my gaze lands on a tattoo of a scrolling letter *B* right over his heart, and I think Megan must be B.

Brittney?

Breanna?

Bailey?

Bethany, I bet. She looks like one.

Megan with a B traces the scrolling letter. For some reason, I can't call her Bethany. To me she's Megan. I'll stick with that. "I'm sorry, Cam. I'm so sorry," she whispers.

"Just shut up," he hisses, and I wish I could see his face so I could tell if he's angry or if he likes to be rough.

My thoughts are soon left in the dust because red soles are all I can see when she drops to her knees. Shocked, I have to use my hand to cover my gasp. This is not what I expected. Either way, it's too late for me to say a word.

Slowly, she unzips the fine fabric of his trousers, and I want to die.

I can't watch this.

Yet, I do.

The pink lights flicker over and around me, and if either of them looks toward the corner, they might catch a glimpse of my extremely bold, large silver zipper. Remind me why I suggested this change to the designer? Inching my way farther back, I make sure to blend in with my all-black attire.

"I want you," she moans with a harsh breath.

"You don't get to have me," he sneers at her.

"How about this, then?" she asks as she strokes his cock, which is still covered by his boxers, and then kisses it.

From the groan he makes, it sounds like he's battling himself. "You don't want to do this," he replies, and something in the sound of his tortured, low, creamy voice sets my blood on fire.

She ignores his response and yanks his pants and boxers past his knees. No pants required for this act. And then without any more preamble, she takes him in her mouth and sheaths him with her lips. I can't see his cock, but that doesn't mean I don't want to.

Really, I'm not a pervert. I'm not even the least bit kinky. In fact, I'm the opposite of kinky. I jill off with my fingers. I like sex missionary style, on a bed, at night, in the dark. And I'm not very good at blowjobs. I usually gag.

There's a dull thud against the door, and I imagine it is Cam tipping his head in pleasure despite the fact that he's mad at Megan with a B.

Why is he mad?

What did she do?

Who is she?

A random pickup?

His girlfriend?

His fiancée?

His wife?

I'm going with girlfriend. I feel like the intimacy she used to trace the letter on his chest meant something. Not fiancée or wife—I don't see rings—but I guess if they are in a fight they might have taken them off. What did she do to upset him? Spend too much money? Get tipsy at lunch? Refuse to spread her legs when he wanted her to?

The act continues. Her long, dark hair bobs. His shirttails practically cover her head. And then his tie whispers across the hint of skin I can see between the folds of fabric, and I start to feel a little overheated. None of that seems to bother her, though, as she works him with both her hands and her mouth.

Up.

Down.

Up.

Down.

My eyes feel dry. I blink them a few times. *Damn contacts.* The movement of my head causes the gemstone around my neck to fall and hit the side of the floor.

Tick.

Tock.

Tick.

Tock.

Like a clock, it moves until I grab it.

Suddenly, B stops what she's doing and looks up at Cam.

Did she hear it?

I stop breathing.

"You like it when I do this. Admit it," she purrs.

Phew. She didn't hear anything.

Angry or not, I know I don't imagine the sound of laughter he makes or the hand he puts on B's hair as he pushes her head down. "In the condition I'm in tonight, sweetheart, any whore will do."

Mean, vicious words meant to hurt, or is this just their way?

The use of the word *sweetheart* tells me he refuses to call her by name. Megan with a B doesn't seem to mind, because soon enough the wet noise of mouth on flesh is the only sound besides my heavy breathing that I can hear.

"Fuck, that's good," Cam groans.

"I know how you like it," B tells him, looking up again.

Okay, so at least they're well acquainted. Again, I'm going with girlfriend.

Cam doesn't seem to want to look into her eyes, because he once again pushes her head down. "Who wouldn't?" he tells her, and for the first time, I hear the slur of alcohol in his voice.

Fascinated by the exchange before me, I'm more than aware that I shouldn't be watching this or listening to this private moment, but I want to know if being an asshole is how he gets off, or if Cam is truly mad at Megan with a B.

A light flickers under the table and I grab for my phone. It's another text from Maggie, same as before.

Maggie: Are you still out?

More soft, wet noises cover up the vibration. Thank God I turned my phone to vibrate earlier. With the screen covered with my palm, I try not to move or even breathe.

Cam is making a lot more noises now. Groaning. Swearing.

Why are his sounds turning me on?

Feeling a way I know I shouldn't, I close my eyes, unable to watch anymore, but soon enough another thud against the door has me opening them just in time to see Cam's back arch.

I know he's coming by the way his body is reacting—the sounds he's making, the curve of his spine, the sudden thrusts he makes into B's mouth. "That's it, right there. Don't stop. Don't stop. Oh, fuck. Oh, fuck."

Megan with a B swallows all of him to the last drop and from what I can see, she doesn't seem to have a gagging issue.

Lucky bitch.

Right now, I'm more than a little hot and bothered. I know what I'll be doing when I get home to relieve the ache I'm feeling.

Megan's arm rises and she wipes her mouth. *I wish I could hand her a napkin.* Soon after, she gets to her feet and I can no longer see anything but the back of her red dress.

She's the devil.

Or maybe he is?

"No," says the very male, very drunk, voice.

No.

No to what?

Oh, God, I hope she doesn't want to lay him down on the floor and fuck him, because if that happens, I'm so caught.

"No?" Megan with a B repeats in a questioning tone.

"No!"

"Wait. Let me get this straight—you'll let me suck your dick, but you won't let me touch your mouth with my lips?"

Cam's polished shoes shuffle. He pulls his shirt together. Tucks it. Zips his pants. Then he moves away from the red dress in the high heels and opens the door. "I'm done letting you do anything else, sweetheart."

Well, that is just rude.

"Camden," she calls, sounding a little frantic. "Give me a chance. I want to make it up to you. I'll do anything."

"There's nothing I want from you—that's the problem."

Cam. Short for Camden.

I rather like it.

Too bad Camden is a prick.

"Then why let me do this?"

There is no answer, just his feet moving out of my sight.

"You're a fucking asshole!" she cries after him.

Those polished, very male shoes come flying into the room.

Hell hath no fury like a man scorned.

He steps very close to her. I imagine him tipping her chin up to look her in the eyes, although I can't see up that high. "Just so we're clear on this—I owe you nothing," he seethes, and this time when he leaves the room he doesn't return.

Ouch!

"But I still want you," she whispers, more to herself.

I think she's used to getting what she wants, and this Cam is it. I wonder how far she'll go to get him. Wish I could find out.

Soon after, Megan with a B stumbles, and then slumps onto the bench at the table across from me. I can see her face now.

Oh, God.

Oh, God.

Please don't look this way.

If I can see her face, does that mean she can see mine?

It's dark enough in the corner and I hope the glow of the pink lights helps to camouflage me, but if she looks hard enough, she'll see me.

Sadness consumes her and her crying is as heavy as her breathing. She's not looking anywhere but into her own lap. I feel a little sorry for her. I don't know what she did to Camden, but it must have been very bad, or this is one really fucked-up sex game they're playing.

Too bad for me I will probably never know because as if reborn, she wipes the tears from her eyes, takes a deep breath, and stands tall before she walks out of the room with a very steady stride.

Boy, does she put herself together quickly.

I could take a page or two from her "how to" book.

Hard to believe I just did that—watched a girl give a guy a blow-job. Honestly, I didn't see much, just the back of her head, but still, that has to count as anything but uptight.

Right?

When the coast is clear, I grab my phone, finally press send with the one word, *yes*, to answer Maggie, and make my way into the lounge. There is no sign of Megan with a B, and although I'm uncertain what Cam looks like, something tells me he's gone too.

"Happy" is playing and my friends are onstage moving like Pharrell Williams. Practically skipping toward them, I hop up and join in. Moving my hips, snapping my fingers, clapping my hands, I have no trouble belting out this tune all the way through.

"Clap along, if you feel like that's what . . ." I finish the song on a high note, with my hands together and a sense of being reborn myself.

What I watched in that private room makes me realize everyone has issues, and everyone has a way of dealing with them—beg, cry, get mad, say things that hurt, curl up into a ball, and even have sex. However you deal, at least you deal, and I've done my fair share of all of that.

I'm done dealing.

I'm ready for tomorrow.

Ready to start anew.

Be a hot-air balloon, just like the song says.

Within minutes of our grand finale, I'm drunkenly hugging my friends goodbye.

"Don't forget to call us!" they holler as I get into a cab.

"I won't," I answer, closing the window, and then turning around to wave goodbye as the taxi pulls away.

Slumping against the door, reality dawns. In less than twenty-four hours, I'll be on a plane to Orange County.

I can't believe it.

I'm really doing it.

New start.

New life.

New me.

California, here I come.

About the Author

KIM KARR IS a *New York Times* and *USA Today* bestselling author.

She grew up in Rochester, New York, and now lives in Florida with her husband and four kids. She's always had a love for reading books and writing. Being an English major in college, she wanted to teach at the college level, but that was not to be. She went on to receive an MBA and became a project manager until quitting to raise her family. Kim currently works part-time with her husband and recently decided to embrace one of her biggest passions—writing.

Kim wears a lot of hats: writer, book-lover, wife, soccer mom, taxi driver, and the all-around go-to person of her family. However, she always finds time to read. One of her favorite family outings when her kids were little was taking them to the bookstore or the library. Today, Kim's oldest child is twenty-one and no longer goes with her on these now rare and infrequent outings. She finds that she doesn't need to go on them anymore because she has the greatest device ever invented—a Kindle.

Kim likes to believe in soul mates, kindred spirits, true friends, and happily-ever-afters. She loves to drink champagne and listen to music, and hopes to always stay young at heart.

www.authorkimkarr.com
Facebook, Twitter, Instagram, Amazon

also by

NEW YORK TIMES BESTSELLING AUTHOR

Kim Karr

HOLLYWOOD PRINCE

BEDWRECKER

NO PANTS REQUIRED

THE SET UP

TURN IT UP

SET THE PACE

TAINTED LOVE

BLOW

CRUSH

TOXIC

THE 27 CLUB

FRAYED

BLURRED

MENDED

DAZED

TORN

CONNECTED

Made in the USA
Lexington, KY
30 June 2017